Willard Glover Nash

A century of gossip or the real and the seeming by Willard G. Nash

Willard Glover Nash

A century of gossip or the real and the seeming by Willard G. Nash

ISBN/EAN: 9783743367753

Manufactured in Europe, USA, Canada, Australia, Japa

Cover: Foto ©Andreas Hilbeck / pixelio.de

Manufactured and distributed by brebook publishing software (www.brebook.com)

Willard Glover Nash

A century of gossip or the real and the seeming by Willard G. Nash

He injured his voice pleading at the bar   They look at his face and "guess the bar-keeper must have been very deaf."—PAGE 332.

NEW ENGLAND LIFE.

A

CENTURY OF GOSSIP.

OR,

THE REAL AND THE SEEMING.

By WILLARD G. NASH.

CHICAGO:
W. B. KEEN, COOKE & CO.
1876.

CONTENTS.

A CENTURY OF GOSSIP.

CHAPTER I.

UNCLE HENRY.

NO New England village is complete without a shoe shop. It is the place of resort for old and young; the "home," where male gossips love to congregate in the evening and pass around the tit-bits of scandal that have been gathered during the day. Bits of scandal never grow less by being passed around in a shoe shop; and in this respect scandal is unlike a plug of tobacco, 'though both are pernicious. There are in New England many noble men whose homes are brightened and gladdened by that gentle and refining influence that a good man never fails to exert; men who — not cursed by lands or gold — are rich in all that makes life desirable; but they do not spend their evenings in a shoe shop. They regard life as too short to be frittered away in worse than idle talk, too precious to be spent in retailing scandal; and yet one sometimes hears good things in a shoe shop. Among the mass of chaff a few grains of wheat are found.

The shoe shop at Elton village is a venerable structure that has withstood the storms of many seasons. Whether it was built immediately before, or after, the Declaration of Independence was signed, is still an open question, which is discussed with a great deal of animation on each recurring Fourth of July. Uncle Henry, the proprietor, stoutly maintains that it was built by the red men, early in the eighteenth century, and that its red front had grown gray with age when he first entered it, sixty years ago. The reader may regard Uncle Henry's story as an old man's dream, but, in this locality, his veracity is undoubted. Men seldom lie without a motive, and there is nothing to induce Uncle Henry to lie about so simple a thing as the age of his little weather-beaten shoe shop; therefore, the writer believes that it was built by the Indians, and has been the popular resort for Elton gossips for more than a hundred years.

A hundred years! How many hearts have bled in consequence of innuendoes born and nurtured within those walls, and sent forth on their errand of death. To-day, as a hundred years ago, the shaft of malice seeks its victim with unerring flight, blights like the deadly upas, and consigns the innocent to an unhonored grave.

A hundred years! And the little shoe shop remains unchanged, save that wide maple boards have taken the place of the puncheon floor, and the little sapling at the northeast corner has grown to a stately elm, where the robin builds her nest in the early spring time. It is well for the mother bird that her brood cannot understand a word of the scandal that poisons the air they breathe.

Uncle Henry is not a scandal monger, and seldom participates even in the less harmful gossip to which he is nightly compelled to listen. Why don't he stop it? Simply because all New England villagers recognize the right of the gossips to congregate at the shoe shop. Can a strong-minded woman suppress the sewing circle? Can the President of the United States abolish the writ of *habeas corpus?* The responsibility would be light compared with an attempt to exclude the gossips from a shoe shop in a small village. Uncle Henry works on his farm four months of the year—a genuine Coast-of-Maine farm, the products of which give little trouble to the tax assessor; they are all summed up under the two headings, "Tons of Hay," and "Bushels of Potatoes." True, the crop might be cultivated and gathered in four weeks, but Uncle Henry is a philosopher. He profits by the teachings of "Farming Made Easy," and maintains that "the harder a man works on a Coast-of-Maine farm the worse he is off." His stock consists of a horse, two cows, a yearling calf, and a pig, and he is content to work four months on the farm to get them hay and potatoes, and the rest of the time in the shop, to provide meal for their sustenance; and, in this respect, he is not unlike other farmers in this locality, who labor eight months of the year in the ship yards, or elsewhere, in order that they may "keep up the place." The old man is honest, frugal, and strictly orthodox, adhering to the teachings of his ancestors, and having "no faith in these new-fangled ways of crimping boots or getting to Heaven," regarding both as devices of the devil — one to rob men of their money, and the other to cheat them of their souls. Crimping machines, liberal theology, and oak-tanned sole leather, comprise the list of his abominations. He will not place his soul in jeopardy by putting an oak-tanned sole on a stoga boot; and there is something that borders on the sublime in his devotion to the Baptist creed and hemlock tan. His father believed in the efficacy of cold water and hemlock bark, and why should the son reject the creed of the father? Who shall say that in this he has not chosen the wiser part? In view of the liberalism of the nineteenth century — which verges on unbridled license — is it not well to ingraft a little of the faith of our fathers into the theological tree? Its growth may be retarded, yet it will bear better fruit. But the " liberalism " of the nineteenth century is not confined to theology. Appropriating to our own use the property of another is simply a " little irregularity," and downright, old-fashioned stealing is "embezzling." The murderer goes unwhipped of justice, because modern science, stimulated by liberalism, pronounces him temporarily insane. The man who steals a sheep has "engaged in the mutton business," and a gambler is a dealer in pasteboard and ivory. The government official whose accounts show a deficit of a few thousand dollars, merely "got the best of Uncle Sam in that little financial transaction." Under the magnifying influence of our unbounded liberalism, the quack succeeds the educated physician, and brass commands a premium while brains are discounted.

Liberalism is demoralizing political parties. The wise men, to whom we looked for counsel and advice, have been superseded by self-constituted leaders, who have not learned the alphabet of political economy. Under their management party conventions are not deliberative bodies; they are simply the meetings of the mob to reward unlimited cheek and ignore worth and merit. It will be well for the people when they learn to distinguish between the real and the seeming, and open their eyes to the impracticability of stocking a tan-yard with a shoe-string.

These new ideas about religious, political, and social life are not "fellowshipped" by Uncle Henry. He does not believe in "ideas." He knows how to do honest work, understands the multiplication table, and is familiar with the writings of St. Paul; but he never tried to fathom the mystery of the Credit Mobilier, or solve the financial problem. His theory is, that a shoemaker should stick to his last, and it will last him all his life. His shop contains two shoe benches, a chair, a stove and two long seats placed at the sides, for the accommodation of numerous visitors. He locks his shop; not because it contains articles of value, but he do n't want to apologize for the absence of such articles if a thief should happen to break in. Men dislike to apologize. A fop will step on the trail of a lady's dress and make what he is pleased to term a graceful apology, but a true man always regrets the necessity, and performs the unpleasant task much as a schoolboy submits to his first flogging — from a sense of duty.

"A fine evening, Uncle Henry." And Philip, the philosopher, sat down on the vacant chair, stretched his long legs under the high stove,

took in a bountiful supply of the Virginia weed,
and prepared to enjoy a quiet evening with the
venerable shoemaker. It was a bitter cold night,
and Philip "calculated" that the gossips would
not venture out. Our philosopher does not like
the gossips. "If you can't speak well of a man,
hold your tongue," is his motto, and it would be
well if the world would adopt it. Philip is content to enjoy the world as he found it, knowing
full well that he cannot reform even so small a
part of it as Elton village. Armed with a clay
pipe, a plug of tobacco, a card of matches, and
his old flint-lock rifle, he can spend a day in the
woods wholly unmindful of the supply of wood
at home. The dream of a genuine philosopher
is never disturbed by the size of the wood pile,
or the condition of the flour barrel. Philip is a
patient and persistent hunter, but he never gets
any game, except an occasional game of whist
won at a sitting with the village parson, who has
not outgrown a fondness for that branch of his
schoolboy studies. Our philosopher is too kind-
hearted to kill anything. He "drew bead" on
a fine doe, last fall, when her fawn came up, and
he lowered his gun, with the remark, "I can't

make an orphan of that beautiful fawn; I'll go without venison first." As the mother deer bounded away, accompanied by her graceful fawn, a robin sang a sweet carol, which went straight to Philip's heart, and he thanked God that he had not disturbed the winged blessing by an ill-timed shot.

"A fine evening, Uncle Henry, but it will rain to-morrow."

"How do you know?"

"The water bubbles up through the ice on the ponds. A sure sign of rain."

"Your sign will fail this time, Philip. 'T is too cold to rain."

"I know it is cold. As the tide ebbed to-day, the ice in the river creaked and sounded colder than anything I ever heard, except a hypocrite's prayer, but it will rain for all that. The weather changes this winter quicker than a politician can change his tactics."

"Does the prayer of a hypocrite sound so very cold to you?"

"Yes, sort o' coolish, Uncle Henry. There, is no heart in a hypocrite's prayer. When my Joe runs away from school, and lies to me about it, his voice almost freezes me; and when I hear a hypocrite pray, it always reminds me of Joe's lies, and I want to get near the fire."

"If I did n't know your habits so well, I should guess that you had been up on the hill, listening to one of Deacon Wells' prayers. Your description is complete."

"I never heard the Deacon pray. All I know about him is what I hear from the boys in here, and 't aint always safe to bet on the boys, you know."

"Not always, Philip, but boys form wonderfully correct opinions about men, and they generally speak the truth."

"Yes; 'though they are quite apt to jump at conclusions."

"While men hesitate, ponder, and get lost in the fog."

"Is n't it well to 'hesitate and ponder' before passing judgment on a man's character? The great want of the age is a want of charity. We judge men harshly, magnifying the evil and losing sight of the good that is in them. While men do not 'hesitate and ponder' as much as they should, boys form their opinions of character, as of everything else, from impulse, and do n't reason at all; so, 'taint always safe to bet on the boys."

" I 'd sooner risk a boy's instinct than a man's reason, on the question of character. The Almighty writes a plain hand, and boys read it more readily than men."

" What has God written on the face of Deacon Wells, that you should pronounce him a hypocrite? "

" What has he not written there? His little sunken, snake-like eyes, thin lips, low forehead, and sharp chin, all bear evidence of his cold-heartedness, and a cold-hearted man can 't be a Christian."

" Parson Green has small, sunken eyes, thin lips, and a low forehead. Is he a hypocrite? "

Here was a dilemma. Uncle Henry greatly disliked Deacon Wells, who spent much of his time in the shoe shop, and the old man never detected his striking resemblance to Parson Green. The Parson is a true Christian, kind, liberal, and devoted to his people. For many years he has ministered to the spiritual wants of the parish. Philip and Uncle Henry echo the

sentiments of all his people when they pronounce him "the best man on the coast of
Maine." His charity is unbounded. On his
first Sunday in Elton, his prayer that "all men
might be saved," startled a few of the old cast-
iron pillars of the church, and they "feared he
wan't sound on doctrinal pints," but he has
won them over, by his pure life and gentle
teachings, and they, long ago, ceased to look for
something to condemn in Parson Green. "Does
he believe in the orthodox hell?" That question, kind reader, can be answered only by the
Parson. He does not portray its horrors to the
young men of Elton in order to frighten them
into a pretended worship of the Divine Master.
He does not teach that cringing fear of hell will
fit a man for Heaven. He is content to teach
his people that "God is love," and dwell on His
protecting care, leaving others — to whom the
task is congenial — to tell of His vengeance and
His hate. He reads with pleasure and indorses
much of "Collier's Every-day Subjects in Sunday Sermons," and thinks "Talmage's Abominations" well named. Parson Green never
wears a long face, except on funeral occasions,

and then it requires all his self-control to keep his facial muscles properly elongated. If the deceased brother's soul is in Heaven, why should the pastor look so sad about it? This question always torments him at a funeral. He is a sunny Christian, who believes in scattering sunshine wherever he goes. He has taught the fathers and mothers in Israel to look cheerful — instead of weeping — when they relate their "experience" at the monthly conference meeting. Under his genial influence, the young folks have substituted "Charades" and "Authors" for "Copenhagen" and "Chase the Squirrel." The boys do not swear on the base-ball ground, for our Parson is always there — the best bat among them. The young people love him, and he gathers them into the fold. A prayer in the village of Elton is not complete unless it concludes with "God bless our Parson Green." Will not God bless him who so richly blesses his fellow man? "For whosoever hath, to him shall be given, and he shall have more abundance." It would be well for the morals of the nation if every ward and village could boast of a Parson Green. He does not attempt to plow the barren fields of narrow orthodoxy, nor does he cultivate the noxious weeds of a dangerous liberalism. No man in the village has a warmer friendship for the Parson than Uncle Henry, and when Philip asked the question, the old man drove the pegs with increased vigor for a moment, and replied:

"Much as I dislike gossip, I can't refrain from expressing my opinion of Deacon Wells. It is sacrilege for you to mention the two in the same breath. They have not the same expression, by a long shot, and the Deacon's headpiece don't begin with the Parson's."

"No; but their features are alike; which simply proves that we can't read God's handwriting."

"Well, there's a good deal in it, Philip. Of course there are exceptions to all rules. You can't find a striped squirrel in every hollow fence pole, but that is the place to look for them."

"Yes; and studying physiognomy is much like hunting striped squirrels. It does n't pay for the time wasted."

"That depends. If a man is fond of striped

squirrels, it pays to hunt them; and if he has a taste for physiognomy, it pays to study it."

"And, after he has studied for years, reject it on account of the 'exceptions'? The idea that the 'exception proves the rule' won't do. Fixed rules, only, are worthy of confidence. There are too many 'exceptions' in physiognomy."

"There you are treading on dangerous ground, my boy. No fact is better established than that 'there are exceptions to all general rules.' It is the rule that boys raised under proper influences make good men, but sometimes a preacher's son turns out badly. He is an 'exception'."

"Not necessarily. Preachers' sons are not always raised under 'proper influences.' There is often a wide difference between the private and public life of a preacher — a difference which boys readily perceive — and it is this evidence of hypocrisy that makes them 'turn out badly.' If the father is simply a guide-board, the son will take another road than that which is pointed out to him. The devil needs no better servants than men who stand still and point out the way. The few who attempt to follow their directions are soon lost in doubt, and those who know them best are sure to take the other road."

" But a spiritual guideboard is only another 'exception' which proves the rule."

At this point the conversation was interrupted by the entrance of Deacon Wells, who, in spite of the cold, "came in to put a few nails in his boot-heel." Uncle Henry kindly gave him a last, hammer, and nails, knowing full well that the Deacon's object was to save fifteen cents by doing his own cobbling. Not that he might purchase with it the necessaries of life; not that he might give it to the poor, or place it in the missionary box. The Deacon does not lend his money to the Lord. He is saving it to buy the " Jones place," which is to be sold by the Sheriff next week. As Jones — his early friend and benefactor — is dead, and the orphan children have no moneyed friends to assist them, he thinks it "can be bought at a bargain." And so it can; but the devil will be a party to the contract, and he will surely foreclose his mortgage on Deacon Wells. This world would be a paradise, weeded of the Deacon and kindred spirits.

CHAPTER II.

DEACON WELLS.

"PATIENCE, black my best boots, git out my great coat, and patch up this ragged ten cents. I shall be late to conference." And Deacon Wells took from his pocket the county paper — borrowed from a neighbor — and read the advertisement of the Sheriff offering the Bently farm at public auction. Since his purchase of the " Jones place," he has a fondness for that kind of reading matter. He has read that same advertisement a dozen times during the week, but he will read it again, and calculate how many dollars he can realize out of his anticipated " bargain," by way of preparing his mind for conference. He regretted to spare the half-day, for he is the town tax-gatherer — a position for which he is eminently fitted; and were he the county hangman, the " eternal fitness of things" would still be preserved. Like many other tax-gatherers, the Deacon oppresses the poor and lets the rich "pay when they find it convenient," and on that particular Saturday he expected to levy on Widow Brown's cow, and have his son Elijah, the pride of his heart, bid her off for the paltry sum of three dollars and eighty-eight cents; but he must go to conference and tell his "experience."

Tell his experience? God save the mark! Conference meetings would be numbered among the things that were, if men like Deacon Wells should tell what is hidden in their hearts.

The Deacon's family consists of his wife, Patience, and his two sons, Elijah and James. Patience Wells is as broad and noble as her husband is narrow and selfish. The first hour of wedded life taught her that she had made a fatal mistake. A poor orphan, weary of the hardships of her lot, she married for a home. The Deacon studiously concealed his true character during his courtship, and while she knew that she did not love him, she imagined that she could respect and obey, and might "learn to love him in time;" but on the evening of their marriage, when he told her she "must read the Scripter, jine church, and live as a deacon's wife orter," she realized that there was an impassable gulf between them. Joining church was, to her, something more than a mere form, and the command revealed her husband's hypocrisy, chilled her heart, and taught her the sad lesson of his cruel deceit. Bitter, indeed, would be the fruit of her ill-starred marriage, but she would suffer in silence, and in silence she suffers still. She is only one of the great army of unhappy wives, who find, too late, that they cannot " learn to love."

Elijah Wells, the Deacon's first born, is the " improved edition " of his father, who named him " accordin' to Scripter." There is nothing about Elijah that suggests Holy Writ, save his name. His conduct is sadly at variance with its teachings. He is cold, cruel, and grasping ; his father's joy and his mother's great sorrow. All Elton wonders how Patience Wells could bear such a child; but Elton, like the rest of the great world, has not fathomed the mysteries of hereditary transmission.

James, the younger, is the opposite of his

" Patience, black my best boots, get out my great coat, and patch up this ragged ten cents."—PAGE 22.

brother. He has the broad, high forehead, and full, hazel eyes of his mother, and has inherited many of her excellent traits of character; but, unlike her, he will not tamely submit to the tyranny of his father and brother. By the persistent effort of his mother he has been kept at school for several years, has access to the law library of an attorney in a neighboring village, and is preparing to enter a profession in which he is destined to make his mark.

"Come, Patience, hurry up. I must be there in time. A deacon orter let his light shine, and not hide it under a bushel. (Or a peck measure, thought his doubting wife, but she dared not utter her thoughts.) And I want to get through in time to levy on Widow Brown's cow, if I can. If I give her time, she'll raise the heft of her tax by sellin' socks, and some meddlin' neighbor will lend her the rest, and I will miss that cow."

"Has Widow Brown more than one cow?"

"Only one. She sold the other to pay her husband's funeral expenses."

"And do you really want to take advantage

of her necessities, and — buy her only cow for a song?"

"Take advantage of her needcessities? What a fool you air, Patience. It is my duty to collect the taxes, and I allers try to do my duty."

"Why don't you collect the tax of Esquire Gould? The amount is twenty times larger than Widow Brown's."

"That's a hoss of another color, Patience. 'Squire Gould got me my appintment, and I ain't goin' to be ongrateful."

"When, at conference, you ask God to remember the poor, will not thoughts of Widow Brown's cow intrude, and interfere with your devotions?"

"See here, Patience, I've heered enough of that nonsense. The Bible says a man that don't look out for his own household is worse 'n a infidel; and I b'lieve the Bible; there's the difference atwixt us."

"Does not your Bible teach you to care for the widow and the fatherless?"

"Ain't I as much of a orphan as Sam Brown's children? When I'm lookin' out for myself,

I'm obeyin' the Scripteral injunkshun to look out for the fatherless."

"You have enough, and to spare. If you will pay the widow's taxes, instead of rob — taking her cow, God will bless you for the deed."

"You'd better make a confeshun and jine church afore you preach to one of the Lord's anninted. I'm tired of heerin' that nonsense. God blesses the man as looks out for number one; and that's me. You've been learnin' Jim your hifalutin' noshuns 'till you've made him a infidel. He told me to my face that I might as well rob the Widow Brown as to buy her cow for taxes. He said 'rob,' Patience, and that's what comes of your sinful conduct."

"And what reply did you make?"

"I told him he was a moonshiny calf, just like his mother, and didn't know beans when the bag's open. He ain't half so sharp as Elijah."

"I hope he never will be 'sharp' enough to oppress the poor. I do not uphold him in his disrespect for his father, but he has noble impulses."

"Noble fiddlesticks! He has the imperence of the devil, and no more sense than a suckin'

dove. It all comes of your snivelin' and my
yieldin' to your foolish noshun about sendin'
him to skule."

" Very well. I will take the responsibility."

"Yes; but that don't pay the bills, nor make
him a dutiful son, like Elijah."

Deacon Wells hurried off to conference to
thank God that he was "not as other men."
Patience went to her room to weep. Never
before had she dared to express her opinion so
freely in her husband's presence. She was ter-
rified by her own boldness, and sought relief in
woman's great panacea — tears.

Conference did not adjourn in time for the
Deacon to "levy on that cow," and he went
home in an ill humor, and vented his spleen at
the supper table — his usual custom. On Sunday and Monday a snow storm kept him in the
house and shoe shop, but early on Tuesday
morning he started for Widow Brown's. "That
track looks 'mazin'ly like old Charley's," he
mused, as he discovered a horse's track in the
snow; "that left fore shoe is as like it as two
peas in a pod; but it can't be his, for he hain't
been out of the barn sense conference." He

rode on in the bitter cold—a fitting morning for his errand—occasionally thinking of "that hoss track." In due time he reached the humble home of Widow Brown, and entered it without knocking. Deacon Wells never knocks at the doors of the poor. Men of his type cannot be courteous, save in the presence of those who are blessed—or cursed—with wealth.

"Good mornin', Sister Brown. I'm sorry, but my duty compels me to levy on your cow for them taxes."

"You need not take the cow, Deacon. I will pay the tax."

The crafty tax-gatherer could not conceal his disappointment. He coveted that Durham cow, and some "meddler" had foiled him. The widow divined his thoughts, and rather enjoyed his discomfiture.

"Where did you git the money, Sister Brown?"

"That is an impudent question, but I will answer it. God put it into the heart of a man more charitable than you, to furnish me the money."

."All right, Sister Brown. The Bible says that charity begins at home, you know."

"The Bible does not say so; and, if it did, it would not say that it should end at home, as your's does."

"Well, Mis Brown, I pay my taxes and all my other debts. No man can say that I owe him a nine-pence, and there ain't many men can say as much."

"That is simply your duty, and it is not a virtue. Men often do a simple act of justice that the law might enforce, and claim credit for magnanimity, and some men are not very particular as to the manner in which they pay their debts."

"I pay mine in lawful money, Mis Brown."

"Was it all obtained in a lawful manner, Deacon Wells?"

"In course it were. Who dare say 't wan't?"

"Every man, woman, and child, in Elton, except your poor wife, dare say it, Deacon. Even your son James, if pressed, would not deny it. Do you think the Eltonians have forgotten the Jones place?"

"That was a square deal, Mis Brown. The

Sheriff sold it accordin' to law; I bought it accordin' to law, and paid for it in lawful money, accordin' to law, and made ten thousand dollars —"

"According to law; but where does the justice come in? Is it just that Bessie Jones should be compelled to wear her life out by teaching school that you may add to your ill-gotten gains? Is it just that her earnings should be used to support her crippled brother when you honestly owe him five thousand dollars? No, *Deacon* Wells. You have robbed the children of your early friend, and God will surely punish you for it. He will not quite forget sweet Bessie Jones."

"You air a imperent, ungodly woman, and if you was wuth anything, I'd make you prove what you say."

"I shall take pleasure in doing it any time that may suit you, Deacon."

The atmosphere was too warm for Deacon Wells. He took the widow's money, gave her a scrawl which he called a receipt, and started for home, in a very uncomfortable mood. He knew he was a hypocrite, but, until Mrs.

Brown opened his eyes, he imagined he was deceiving all the world except his son Elijah. He even dreamed that he was deceiving Patience and James. It was a terrible awakening for Deacon Wells. Not that his conscience troubled him, but, like other men, he could not regard the opinions of his fellows with indifference. Men, however depraved, never sink so low that public opinion cannot reach them, nor do they rise above it. It governs the conduct of· the statesman, and dictates the utterances of the theologian. It tempts the criminal to go from the gallows with a lie upon his lips, to meet an offended God. It is no wonder that the Deacon was agitated when he learned the verdict of the terrible tribunal. At enmity with all the world, he reached home, determined to "make some-body smart."

" Elijah, has old Charley been out of the barn sense conference?"

"I guess not. Maybe Jim had him out. I hain't used him."

" Where's Jim?"

" Up in the corner bedroom, with his head in them pesky law books."

"Patience, tell Jim to come down here immejiately."

The tired mother sought her son, and delivered the message. She knew the Deacon was very angry, and she asked James to keep cool, and remember that he was to meet and talk with his father. "Above all things, my boy, let your language be courteous and respectful," was her earnest admonition. "I will try, for your sake, dear mother," was his reply, as he went down to the sitting room, firmly resolved to obey; but steel cannot clash with steel without bringing the sparks.

"Jim, have you had old Charley out of the barn sense conference?"

"Yes, sir."

"When?"

"Last evening."

"What did you take him out for?"

"To ride."

"Where?"

"Where I pleased to go, father. I am no longer a child; and, even in childhood, I had the privilege of taking a horse from the stable, and going and returning unquestioned. I have not

3

injured old Charley, nor have I used him for a bad purpose. This assurance ought to suffice."

"But it do n't 'suffice,' my sweet blossom, and if you do n't tell me where you went, and what you went for, I 'll cut you off with a shillin'. If you air too big to larrup, I can fetch you that way."

"All right, father. I accept the alternative."

"Accept the what?"

"The alternative."

"None of your French talk to me, young man. I do n't want none of your frog-eatin' lang-widge. Put it in plain English."

"I mean that I accept your conditions. I will take the shilling, and will not tell you where I went."

"You won't, hey! Your imperence shall cost you fifty thousand dollars. You will wish you had n't turned up your nose at the goose that lays the golden aig. You 'll make a fine lookin' porper, with your soft hands and hifalutin' airs. I wonder if Parson Green's church, that you take such a shine to, will tide you over then?"

"I 'll row my own boat against both wind and tide, if it be necessary; but you need not sneer at Parson Green, or his church. It would be well for you to learn something of pure religion from Parson Green."

"He can learn us base ball, but I want none of his expoundin' of Scripter on doctrinal pints. If you and your mother had kept away from his church, you 'd have understood more about what was becomin' for a deacon's wife and son."

"And less about true Christianity."

"And," interrupted Elijah, "less about shay-rades, and that game of cards with no jacks in it."

James left the room, fearing to remain, lest he might wound his mother by giving free utterance to his thoughts.

"There, mother, is a sample of your Parson Green Christians. Stealin' a hoss out of the barn, and refusin' to tell his dad where he went, may be good religion, but it won't go down with me."

"I am sorry that James did not tell his father where he went with the horse, Elijah, but I am equally sorry to hear you speak so of your brother."

"You 've made a stuck-up fool of him,

mother, with your soft words and high eddi-cashun.”

“ Elijah is right, Patience. If you ’d let me trained him accordin’ to Scripter, and sent him to our church, he ’d been a different kind of a bird’s aig.”

“ Yes, mother, he ’s nothing but a crow’s aig now, and if dad ’ad had the trainin’ of him he ’d a knowd what to do for a sick hoss by this time.”

“ To be shure he would, Elijah; and he ’d a knowd better than to fool away fifty thousand dollars by a little imperence; but it ’s all the better for you, Elijah.”

“ Well, ’t will learn him better than to talk French to you, father, and I guess I know how to take care of the money.”

“ So you do, Elijah; and you help me make it, while Jim does nothin’ but spend it.”

“ He will earn money when he masters his profession. Lawyer Armstrong says he pos-sesses legal ability, and will have a lucrative practice.”

“ What ’s a ‘ lucrative practice,’ Patience ? ”

“ Money-making business.”

“And what’s a ‘legal remedy,’ mother?”

“A lawful remedy; but why do you ask?”

“I heered Jack Blunt tell Jim that dad gave him and Tom Siddons fifty dollars apiece for apprisin’ the Jones place for so much less than ’t was wuth; and he told Jim there was no notice served on Bessie Jones, and asked Jim what Bessie could do about it, and Jim told him she had her legal remedy, and I did n’t know what that were, that’s all.”

“It’s enough, I kalkerlate. I’ll make Jack Blunt smart for that. He’s a ongrateful dog to take my money and then blow on me. I’ll fix him the next court. I’ve got a morgidge on his house.”

“Then you’ll have the fat in the fire, father. (It was one of Elijah’s peculiarities to address Deacon Wells as ‘father,’ and speak of him as ‘dad.’) Better let me cozzen up to Bessie Jones and buy her intrust for a new dress; then you can go for Jack Blunt.”

“Your hed’s mighty level, Elijah. That’s the way we’ll do it.”

“What is her interest worth?” asked Patience.

" The place is wuth fifteen thousand dollars. I bought it for five thousand, and made a cool ten thousand in the barg'in. Her half would be held for half of her father's debts, and that would make her intrust wuth five thousand dollars, and Elijah is sharp enough to get her to sign a quit-claim deed for a five-dollar dress. That 's the way we 'll work it."

" It may be ' sharp,' but will it be right? "

" In course it will. Is n't it right for a man to make all the money he can accordin' to law? "

" I cannot see how a transaction so unjust can be lawful."

" Nobody expects you to ' see it,' mother. It 's a good thing for us that wimmin do n't know nothin' about the law."

" If women made the laws they would not be so manifestly unjust, I hope; 'though the fault may be less in the law than in the loose manner of administering it."

" We do n't want to hear no lectur' about wimmin's rights, Patience. You 're allers a harpin' on some nonsense or other. It all comes of Parson Green lettin' wimmin speak in meetin'. He orter know better, for 't ain't Scripteral."

" I have never spoken at any of the meetings of Parson Green's church."

" You 've heered other wimmin speak, and that 's jest as bad. The Bible says wimmin should be seen, not heered."

" You find many very strange things in the Bible."

" In course I do. I read it. If you 'd take the Bible for your guide, as a deacon's wife orter, you 'd know somethin' about ₋men's rights."

" My Bible does not teach that man has the right to defraud a poor orphan of her patrimony."

" Your's is a wimmin's Bible, mother."

" Our conversashun is gittin' scattered, Patience. I want to know if you know where Jim went with old Charley; and, if you know, be you goin' to tell me?"

" I do not know. I presume he went on an errand of mercy. He was, doubtless, acting as becometh the son of a deacon."

" Actin' more like the son of a wimmin's

rights fool, I kalkerlate.　There is preshus little of my blood in his veins."

"God knows I hope you are right, father," said James, as he entered the room, purple with rage.　"The poisonous fluid would blacken my heart."

"James, for my sake, say no more, and leave the room."

"I *must* speak, mother!　You shall no longer submit to their tyranny."

"Shame on you, Jim, to talk that way to your dad."

"This is not your quarrel, Elijah.　I have been an unwilling listener to your conversation, and I have a right to speak.　I will not be silent and let you abuse mother simply because she dares to plead for the right.　I heard your damnable plot to rob Bessie Jones of her interest in her father's place.　Such villainy will not go unpunished, and 'though our laws are defective, they are strong enough to compel you to make restitution.　Justice will some day overtake you, and I tremble when I contemplate the result. Your avarice will lead you to a felon's cell, and your ill-gotten wealth will not unlock its door.

I cannot remain beneath this roof and eat bread that has been stolen from the widow and the orphan. To-day I will go out into the world, and, by honest toil, provide an humble home. You shall go with me, mother, and 'though you cannot be happy, you can be free from this cursed tyranny. You shall no longer be the slave of criminals."

"Nobody do n't want you to stay, Jim. Elijah and me can run the place better without you. You 're a little mite too good for this world, and orter be replanted among the angels, ortent he, Elijah?"

"Yes, father, he orter be planted somewhere; he 's green enough to sprout."

"Do not go away, James. I cannot leave your father, and I cannot live without you."

"I *must* go, mother. I shall feel like a guilty wretch if I remain. Why can you not go with me?"

"Because I promised to 'love, honor and obey' your father. Marriage is a solemn rite, and I shall, at least, obey him."

"Your marriage has, indeed, been 'solemn,' mother. There has been no sunshine in your

life. You cannot 'love,' because you cannot
'honor' Deacon Wells; you can only 'obey,'
and in your case obedience is a crime."

"I do not so regard it, James. My promise
is binding."

"No pledge can bind you, body and soul, to a
man whom you cannot respect. Your life is a
lie, mother, and your marriage is void. In a
matter of such vital importance, every woman
is a law unto herself."

"That is mere sophistry, James. I recognize
no higher marriage law than the statutes of
Maine."

"There *is* a 'higher law,' mother; a law
founded upon the immutable principle of justice
and right; a law that breaks the chains of the
unwilling captive; a law that recognizes alike
the claims of husbands and wives; a law that
annuls all false marriages — the God-given law
of love."

"Our courts do not regard that law, James,
and the world knows no other tribunal."

"The world will honor you if you will be true
to yourself, mother. Go with me, and I will
make you comfortable."

"I do not consider my comfort."

"Go, if you want to, old woman. You've never been what a deacon's wife orter be, and I'm willin'. My doctrine is that there air better fish in the sea than has ever been ketched, and I've got a silver hook to ketch 'em with; eh, Elijah?"

"Yes; but do n't git a young chub, father. Old fish and young uns do n't git along in double harniss."

"It's the young uns that's a botherin' of you, Elijah, you sly dog; but I'll look out for your intrust."

"Never fear, Elijah. I shall not go."

"Good bye, mother dear. You will not forget that I shall have a home for you very soon, and will gladly welcome you."

"I shall not forget, my dear son. The God whom you serve will be with you always, and He shall be unto you more than father, mother, or brother. May His choicest blessings rest on you, my boy."

James left home with a heavy heart, regretting that his mother would not go with him. After his departure, she was subjected to many indignities, and the days were all dark and dreary. There was no one to shield the defense-less wife and mother from the cruel thrusts of a tyrannical husband and a graceless son. She no longer attended Parson Green's church. Even this crumb of comfort was denied her, and she tamely submitted. If the Deacon was foiled in his attempt to rob a widow or an orphan — he preyed only on those whom he thought friend-less — he would go home and "make Patience smart for it"; and the son vied with the father in heaping abuse upon the silent, suffering woman. God is just, and He will, in His own good time, avenge the wrongs that have burned into the soul of Patience Wells.

CHAPTER III.

BESSIE JONES.

"I SHALL go, Harry. The offer is five dollars per month better than any I have received, and Elton is not so far away."

"I don't want you to go to Elton, Bessie. Deacon Wells lives there; and Bob Grant says he cheated you and me out of ten thousand dollars."

"Upon what does he base his conclusions?"

"He says the mill is worth ten thousand dollars, and the timber land five thousand, to say nothing of the farming land, which I admit is not worth much. Deacon Wells bought it all for five thousand dollars. Bob says, if he were an honest man he would pay us five thousand dollars each."

"Robert may be mistaken, dear brother. Deacon Wells is prominent in his church, and if he were dishonest, that would not be."

"Bob says his church believes in total depravity and infant damnation, and he is good enough for a deacon in *such* a church, if he does cheat widows and orphans."

"You should remember, Harry, that Robert's warm friendship for you may lead him into error in his estimate of Deacon Wells. I know the old home place is worth three times the amount it cost him; but Esquire Gray says the sale was in strict accordance with the law, and five thousand dollars was the highest bid."

"It was legal robbery, sister, and your fine reasoning cannot change it. Right is right, and wrong is wrong. The proposition is too plainly written to be misunderstood. The line between right and wrong is well defined, and Deacon Wells knows that he is a thief and a robber."

"That is strong language, Harry, and it pains me to hear you use it."

"It is plain English, Bessie, and 'though I am sorry to grieve you, I cannot retract."

"But you will be just?"

"Aye, when justice is meted out to you. Were it not for these crippled legs, I would not care; but I cannot bear to see you wear your life

out in teaching a village school when a comfortable support is dishonestly withheld."

" I am not 'wearing my life out,' Harry.
Look at my full, red cheeks."

" The result of a month's rest, Bessie. The
roses were not there when you returned from
Glenville."

" The effect of a little trouble at Glenville.
The committee did not sustain me in my efforts
to govern my school. It may never occur
again."

" It will occur again and again, Bessie. So
long as school committees are composed of men
who take no interest in educational matters —
men of neither natural nor acquired ability —
will your ' little trouble' be constantly recurring.
School committees, as at present constituted, are
simply a delusion and a snare. Men fear to do
right, lest they offend an influential neighbor.
There is a world of truth in the homely adage,
that ' kissing goes by favor,' and so long as
there is an appeal to a committee, schools will
be governed on the same principle."

" Boy like, you are jumping at conclusions,
Harry. Some committees are composed of highly

cultivated gentlemen, who feel a deep interest in schools, and manifest a wise discretion in their government."

"They are simply exceptions to the general rule, and are seldom found outside of books."

"I have found them, Harry, and I am not even a primer."

"You are a dear, kind sister, Bessie, and I am a wretched burden to you. I sometimes wish I were dead, that I might no longer be the recipient of your life-destroying bounty."

The orphans wept. Bessie wisely concluded that her poor, deformed brother would find relief in tears, and it was but natural that her's should mingle.

"You are not a burden to me, dear brother. You are all I have to care for, and my life would be very, very lonely without you."

"If I could only work, Bessie, I should be content; but it is so hard to sit here idle and eat the bread you earn by incessant toil."

"You do not consider how much you help me in my studies. What could I do with my Greek were it not for my clever lexicon?"

"But I bring no bread to our table, Bessie."

"You bring richer food for my soul, Harry, and help me beyond your power to calculate."

"I help eat what your bounty provides."

"That is not a fair statement. Every life must have its compensations. To labor for you is one of my 'compensations,' and I am grateful for the privilege."

"Your labor is drudgery, Bessie."

"Far from it, my dear sir. I know no field that I would prefer. Labor is a duty, and I can be more useful as a teacher than in any other vocation."

"There are so many petty annoyances in the life of a school teacher."

"There are 'petty annoyances' in everyone's life. The true philosophy is to rise above them. This is not more difficult in teaching than in any other occupation, and there is a bright side to a school ma'am's life. Her influence over her pupils is felt when they go out into the world to battle for a prominent place upon the stage, and, if it be properly directed, she has her sure reward."

"God will reward you for your self-sacrificing devotion, dear Bessie."

4

"Even in Elton?"

"I hope so, if you must go there; and yet I fear His spirit will not dwell so near the home of Deacon Wells."

"I must go, Harry."

Bessie went.

———

"Where shall I set you down, Miss Jones?"

"At Widow Love's."

"There's where you're wise. She's the best woman on this route, and she's well named, for she loves everybody, even to us poor stage-drivers. Many's the time she's sot up 'till midnight to give me a cup of hot coffee when the thermometer was froze up. I'm not much of a God-fearin' man, for I wa'n't raised that way, but if there is a Heaven, Widow Love will go there, and she'll fly as high as any of the angels, if she does weigh two hundred and forty pounds."

"Thank you. I am glad to learn that she is kind-hearted."

"Kind-hearted is no name for it, Miss Jones. She's kind all over, from the top of her jolly,

round head to the soles of her little, fat feet.
She 'll be a downright mother to you, and
you 'll cry like a baby when you go 'way from
there."

Five-minutes' drive brought them to the
home of Widow Love — a neat little brown
cottage, with a sharp roof and dormer window.
There were no blinds to shut out the sunlight,
and the spotless, white curtains told Bessie that
within, as without, everything was neat and
home-like.

"Come in, dear, and have a cup of hot tea
and a doughnut. You must be thoroughly
chilled by your long ride; and you, too, John.
A cup of tea will do you good."

"Thank you ever so much, Mis Love; but
I 'm jest a leetle behind time to-day, and I
guess I won't stop. I must go into Glenville
on time or bust a trace."

"All right, John. Have your own way, and
break your traces, if you will. There 's no such
thing as making a stage-driver mind."

"If I was n't behind time, I 'd mind you so
quick 't would make your head swim, Mis
Love."

John carried Bessie's trunk to the "best bed-room," mounted the box, touched up his leaders with his Dexter whip, and the Glenville coach went down the hill at a break-neck pace.

"Give me your hat and shawl, Miss Jones, and sit down to your tea. Mine is an humble home, but you are very welcome, and I hope it will seem like home to you."

"Your kindness makes it seem like home already, Mrs. Love."

Widow Love did not reply. She gave Bessie a hearty, motherly kiss, that brought tears of gratitude to the eyes of the orphan; a kiss that lingered on her lips and warmed her heart with joy; a kiss that came to her in dreams, and whispered "All is well."

Bessie's school was much like other village schools. It contained the usual number of bright pupils, as well as the dull and indolent. Two faces, only, attracted particular attention when she entered her school-room. One was that of a pale-faced, bright-eyed boy, with a mass of tangled hair, and a ragged coat and pants; the other a girl of sixteen, with strongly-marked features and a thoughtful expression.

Bessie approached the boy and asked him his name.

"It used to be Robbie Bently, but it's Ragged Bob now."

"Why is it 'Ragged Bob' now?"

"Deacon Wells turned us out of our home, and I am only a bound boy."

Only a bound boy! There is a volume in the sentence. A volume that tells of cold indifference, or cruel neglect. A volume that reveals a selfishness that should make men blush and angels weep. God knows the anguish of the bound boy's heart, but His children are strangely, sadly ignorant, or cruelly unmindful.

During recess, Robbie Bently told the teacher how Deacon Wells had purchased the old homestead at Sheriff's sale, and turned his mother, brother, and four sisters, out into the world. With quivering lip and trembling voice he told of his mother's struggles, sickness, and death. Bessie's heart went out to the poor orphan, and she could but condemn the man whose avarice had caused so much misery. In that hour was born a deep sympathy for the bound boy, that bore rich fruit in his early manhood. The sympathy of a true woman always manifests itself in works; and Bessie Jones is a true woman.

The girl who attracted Bessie's attention was Nellie, only daughter of Jack Blunt. She was modest, intelligent, and fine looking. Her features had none of that doll-baby beauty, that so surely indicates the absence of mental power, but they were marked and attractive. Bessie often observed in her face a far-away look, that told plainly that her mind was not on her books. Was she thinking of her dead mother, whom she remembered as a patient, suffering woman? or was she sorrowing over her father's misdeeds? Her thoughts are sacred, and you and I, kind reader, will not attempt to lift the veil. She knew her mother had grieved over the evil ways of an unworthy, 'though fondly-loved, husband until her tired life went out. She knew that her father, the willing tool of Deacon Wells, had cruelly wronged Bessie Jones. Did she err in withholding that knowledge, when it was in her power to right the wrong the orphan girl was suffering? Was it her duty to consign her father to a felon's cell? Put yourself in her place, and answer the question.

"You 've had a caller, Bessie."

"Who was it, Mrs. Love?"

"Elijah Wells."

"Why did he not come to the school house?"

"He thought you would be home to dinner, in spite of the storm."

"Did he tell you his errand?"

"No, dear. He said he wanted 'a little conversashun with the school mum.' He may be looking for a wife. He's old enough to marry, and if he can find a girl that prefers brass to brains, and will be satisfied with a gizzard, instead of a heart, I should advise him to marry at once."

"Then Mr. Wells is not one of your favorites?"

"Not Elijah, nor the Deacon; but James is one of the best men in the world. He is a lawyer and a Christian — a rare combination."

"Are not most lawyers Christians?"

"That is not my experience, Bessie. I know so many of them that practice little deceptions for their clients. A desire to succeed in their profession too often induces them to distort facts and defeat the ends of justice. They consider it unprofessional to lie, but they will permit a witness to do it for them. There was Lawyer Giles, of Glenville, who tried to collect a note my husband paid in his life-time. He admitted to me that he knew his client was swearing falsely, and when I asked him why he did n't stop him, he said it would have been unprofessional. But for James Wells' cross-examination, I would have had to pay that note, and my little home would have been taken from me. I wish you had heard James' plea. It made the judge, jury, and all the spectators weep, and the jury rendered a verdict without leaving their seats."

" Then you consider James a good lawyer?"

" The best in the State of Maine; and he 's a good Christian, too. He would not take a penny for his services, and he worked very hard to save my home. I made him a dozen fine shirts, and knit him ten pairs of socks, and could hardly induce him to accept even that small fee."

" I presume, Mrs. Love, there are many other Christian gentlemen in the profession. Among my acquaintances are several excellent men, honest, liberal, and philanthropic, who are prominent lawyers. I think real lawyers are truthful, and only the shams do the pettifogging."

"But the 'shams' are largely in the majority — like the quacks in the medical profession."

"Pardon me for differing with you again, Mrs. Love. I do not think the quacks are in the majority in the profession of medicine. A quack makes more noise than a dozen educated physicians, and this noise misleads us in our comparison."

"I hope you are right, Bessie. You have seen more of the world and read more than I, and your opportunities for forming a correct opinion have been better than mine."

"I have not advanced beyond the alphabet in reading, and I know very little of the world."

At this point the conversation was interrupted by the sound of the door-bell. Mrs. Love answered the summons, admitted and introduced Elijah Wells.

"The weather is sort o' coolish, like, Miss Jones."

"Yes, sir; it has been very cold to-day."

"It's good weather for lumberin', and that's a object in this neck o' woods."

"I presume so."

"How do you like your skule?"

"I cannot tell. I have been teaching only one day."

"Yes, mum; but a body finds out a good deal in one day, 'specially in Elton."

"I like your people very much, so far as I know them."

"Yes, Miss Jones; we have a few good people here, but they 're mostly a shiftless set, and they do n't know how to git forehanded in the world."

"Perhaps they think that getting money is not the chief end of life."

"If it is, they 'll never see the chief end, Miss Jones, for they do n't know nothin' about gittin' money. Sense you 've interduced the subject, I 'll tell you what I 've come for. My dad, Deacon Wells, bought your dad's place at Sheriff's sale. You have no intrust in it whatsomever, but I 've brought a quit-claim deed for you to sign, jest to make the title look a little better on the records. If you 'll sign it, I 'll give you a five-dollar dress; that 'll be clear gain."

"If I have no interest in the place, why should I sign your deed?"

"Jest as I said afore; to make it look a little better on the county records; and you make a five-dollar dress, slick and clean."

"I am not an object of charity, Mr. Wells, and if I have nothing to convey, I shall not accept a consideration for signing the deed. I will have the matter examined by a competent attorney, and if it be true that I have no interest in the old homestead I will cheerfully sign the deed without compensation, and you can give the dress to some one who needs it more than I do."

"All right. Let 'Squire Gray examine the thing. He's good enough lawyer to look up titles, and he does a deal of it. Tell him I'll pay the shot."

"Thank you. I will pay my own attorney."

"Will you git 'Squire Gray?"

"I cannot say; I shall think about it."

"Good night, Miss Jones. I'll stick to your takin' the dress, if 'Squire Gray does say you hain't no intrust in the place, which he ondoubtedly will."

"Good evening, Mr. Wells."

Kind-hearted Mrs. Love could with difficulty restrain her joy until Elijah departed.

"Thank the Lord, dearie, you are not penniless. You are worth five thousand dollars this blessed minute."

"Why do you think so?"

"Simply because Deacon Wells and his hopeful son are not around giving away five-dollar dresses. Depend upon it, you still have your interest in the old place, and this is one of his rascally tricks to get you to convey it for a song."

"I dare not hope for such good fortune, Mrs. Love; but I will have a lawyer look into the matter for me."

"Get James Wells. He will do it well, and he will be very moderate in his charges."

"I cannot expect a son to conduct a case against his father; and I have never met Mr. Wells."

"That won't make a mite of difference. They say he left home because he was disgusted with his father's habit of cheating widows and orphans."

"Even if he should consent, it would place him in an extremely embarrassing position. I cannot ask him to do it."

"Maybe you are right, as usual, Bessie. But don't get Esquire Gray to attend to it. Deacon Wells will have him doctored before to-morrow night."

"No, I will not employ Esquire Gray, 'though I have considered him an honest man."

"When you see a man hobnobbing with Deacon Wells as much as Esquire Gray does, he will bear watching. 'Birds of a feather,' you know; and it is safe to judge men by the company they keep."

"I will consult lawyer Ainsworth. I know he is honest and truthful."

———

"That cock won't fight, father. Guess Bessie Jones has lots of good clothes left over. She would n't nibble at that dress."

"What did she say?"

"She kind o' turned up her pink and wite nose, and said she was n't a object of charity."

"Did you tell her she had no intrust whatsomever in the place?"

"Yes. I told her everything you told me to, and a lot on my own hook, besides."

"Well, what's to be done about it?"

"She's goin' to see a lawyer, and I reckomended 'Squire Gray."

"That's right, Elijah. I'll go and see 'Squire Gray to-morrer, and he'll counsel her to sign the deed."

"Can you 'fix him'?"

"He's already fixed. He'll do anything I want him to."

"S'posin' Bessie do n't go to 'Squire Gray?"

"I've tho't it all over, Elijah. If she do n't go to 'Squire Gray, you must kitten up to her and marry her."

"Good enough."

A week after the foregoing conversation, Deacon Wells called his son:

"You must put on yer go-to-meetin'-best and go down to see Bessie Jones this evenin'. She did n't go to 'Squire Gray."

"How do you know?"

"I put Jack Blunt on her track. Last Saturday she went to Glenville, and was in Lawyer Ainsworth's office nearly a hour; so she's got him, and the fat's in the fire, onless you marry the gal; and it's the easiest way to make five thousand dollars."

"But s'posin' Bessie should object?"

"Tell her I'm wuth a cool hundred thousand dollars, and you air my only inheritanser. That'll fetch her quicker'n you can say Jack Roberson."

"So 't will."

"Good evenin', Miss Jones. Tho't I'd drop in and spend the evenin' with you, if you're disengaged."

"Thank you. I have a little work to do, but it will not require all the evening."

"Teechin' skule is sort o' workish bizness, ain't it?"

"Yes, sir. It is laborious, but it has its compensations."

"Has its what?"

"Its compensations."

'Yes, I s'pose so; but they did n't study 'em

when I went to skule. They had n't got that fur
along."

" What were your principal studies?"

" Readin', ritin' and 'rithmetick. I got as
fur as desolate frackshuns in 'rithmetick."

" Then you did not get into algebra?"

" No, mum; but I got into a row with the
master, and walloped him for sayin' my edikashun wan't complete."

" Did you not whip him on a very slight pro-
vocation?"

"I did n't wallop him on a provokashun. I
took him on the skule-house floor. He had no
bizness to say my edikashun wan't complete.
Accordin' to my idee, readin', ritin', and 'rithmetick is enough for anybody. The fellers that
is allers hankerin' after the higher limbs never
make any money."

" But the higher branches are taught in our
common schools, now."

" In our uncommon skules, you orter say, Miss
Jones. It 's them hifalutin' things that makes
our taxes so steep."

" I hope you do not object to paying your
school tax, Mr. Wells?"

“What 's the use of objectin'. Taxes is taxes, and they has to be paid, but the men who want their boys to know it all, pay preshus little taxes.”

“You are familiar with the tax list, are you not?” asked Mrs. Love.

“I s'pose you mean that I know somethin' about it?”

“Yes, sir.”

“I kalkerlate I do. I know nearly every man's tax in the town.”

“Who is the heaviest tax-payer?”

“Deacon Hezekiah Wells pays the most money, but he ain't as heavy as Doctor Smith by nigh onto forty pounds.”

“Then the Deacon is wealthy?”

“No, Mis Love. He is n't a bit stuck up, but he 's well heeled, and his wallet do n't look like the last run o' shad.”

“And he is n't very particular about his manner of filling it, is he?”

“Yes, mum. He 's orful partickeler. He puts the hundreds in one place, the fiftys in another, the twentys in another, the tens in another, and the fives and twos and ones in his little wallet by theirselves.”

“ Does he allow you a liberal supply of spending money?”

“ I do n't go down on my dad for spendin’ money, Mis Love. I have a wallet of my own, and ’t ain’t so lean as a sick hoss, nuther. I speckerlate purty considerble on my own hook. Last week I bought ten yearlin’s and a clam priv’lege.”

“ What will you do with your yearlings?”

“ Sell ’em to the butcher when he gits short.”

“ And the clam privilege?”

“ I ’ll lay low about that ’till some feller gits to diggin’ clams on it, and if he do n’t come down with somethin’ hansum, I ’ll prosecute him for trespass.”

“ Is n’t that a disreputable way of making money, Elijah?”

“ What kind of a way, Mis Love?”

“ A bad way.”

“ No, I guess not. I can make it faster that way than choppin’ cord-wood, or peelin’ hemlock bark, and I allers had a poor appertite for cuttin’ wood.”

“ You cut wood for your mother, do n’t you?”

"I cut considerble sense Jim left; but she burns chips a most of the time."

"Your mother is a dear, good woman, Mr. Wells."

"Yes, mum. She 's sort o' goodish. She 's a tip-top cook and a spankin' good butter-maker; but she keeps sich a hankerin' after Jim that it spiles her for a mother. Dad wants me to kitten up to some good gal and git marrid on the two-forty, and sense I think of it, Miss Jones, you and I would make a hull team, if it 's agreeable to you? "

"I have no desire to change my condition."

"Bless your sweet life, you need n't change nothin' but your name. You can keep right along with your skule, and be earnin' somethin' that way, if you want to. There 'll be no need-cessity for you to work, onless you want to, for dad is wuth a cool hundred thousand, and I 'm his only inheritanser."

"I must decline the honor, Mr. Wells. I do not wish to marry at present."

"You do n't want to git marrid ? Well, Miss Jones, you 're the only gal in Elton that sails on that tack, and you do n't carry sich a tarnashun site of canvas, nuther. The sea is full of fust rate fish, and I 've got a gold hook to ketch 'em with; so, good evenin', Miss Jones."

"Good night, Mr. Wells."

As soon as the door closed, Mrs. Love indulged in a hearty laugh, at the expense of the parsimonious lover.

"Did you ever, Bessie? He is a bigger fool than I supposed him to be."

"You must be charitable, Mrs. Love. Perhaps he inherited his peculiarities."

"So he did. I 'm glad James is like his mother."

———

"The jig 's up, father, and you 'll have to come down with that five-thousand-dollar dust. Bessie Jones mittened me last evenin'."

"Did you tell her what I was wuth?"

"Yes, sir; and I told her I 'd git it all. And I told her I had a wallet of my own, and understood readin', ritin', and 'rithmetick. I told her she need n't work a lick, onless she was a mind to. I tho't I 'd tell her that ontil we was marrid, you know."

"And she sacked you square?"

"That's jest what she did."

"She's a born fool."

"Jess so."

"I won't 'come down with the dust,' Elijah. I've got another plan in my head. Five thousand is wuth playin' for, and I'll win. The man 'at plays Hezekiah Wells for a fool is jest a leetle looney, that's all."

"Shure's you're born; but what's your little game, father?"

"I'll not show my hand jest yet, Elijah."

"Be shure and hold the four aces when you come to a show, father."

"I'll have a hull pack, if it's needful."

CHAPTER IV.

THE GOSSIPS AND OTHERS.

HOORAH for Jim Wells. He 's got the nominashun, and I 'll bait a last year's bird's nest he 'll go to Congress! "

" Is the old Deacon very angry ? "

" Angry ? He 's bilin' over. He put in his oar for 'Squire Gray; but the 'Squire can 't represent this deestrict. He 's too milk-and-waterish. I cum purty near speakin' right in meetin' and tellin' 'em that Elton would n't pull a rope for him, if he got the nominashun."

" Was Jim Wells there ? "

" No; he 's 'tendin' court to Augusta."

" How did he get the nomination ? Conventions do not usually select the best men."

" Why, you see, the other feller that 's runnin' lives at Glenville, and the candidate must come from this end of the deestrict. There was nobody up but him and 'Squire Gray. The old Deacon made a speech agin Jim, and said he was too young and unexperienced to go to Congress. He wan't sharp enough to see that the convenshun was made up of us young fellers, and his speech settled the hash and nominated Jim. Of course it ain't nateral for young fellers to wait 'till they're gray before they can go to Congress; and the 'Squire is Gray and can't go. Hoorah for Jim Wells."

" I hope he will accept the nomination. He would make his mark in Congress."

" Make his mark? He can write as plain a hand as any man in Maine."

" I mean that he will distinguish himself."

" Oh, yes. And he 'll repeal the game law, so a feller can git a little deer meat after the fust of January."

" Exactly; and it would be dear meat if you should hunt 'till you found one."

" 'Tain't your mix, Zach Brown. But I did come purty near killin' one last winter."

" How near? "

" I was jest gittin' ready to fire when he see me and started."

"If you 'd fired that old blunderbus of your's, Uncle Jo West would have been scouring the country, looking for a lost boy."

"That 's so, Zach.　His old gun kicks worse than a blue-nosed mule."

"I notice you 're all glad to git her in rabbit time."

"That 's because we have some sympathy for the rabbits."

Here the conversation was interrupted by the entrance of Elijah Wells, who was not popular with the boys at Elton, and did not feel "at home" in the shoe shop.　He came on business.

"Uncle Henry, I want you to measure my foot for a pair of boots.　I want 'em dirt cheap, and must have 'em right off."

"All right."

"Do n't make 'em, Uncle Henry."

"Why not?"

"Your lasts are all too small, and you will have to make 'em on the turn of the road. There 's a fine for obstructing the highway."

"If I did n't pay no more road tax than you do, Zach Brown, I would n't say much about fines."

" What I do pay is honestly earned, Lige. I wish I could say as much for you."

" You can, if you 'll stick to the truth, and not lie about it."

" See here, Lige. You 're not the man to talk about tellin' the truth. If I owed the devil a thousand liars, and he would n't take you for the debt, I 'd cheat him out of it."

" You ain't sharp enough to cheat anybody, Zach."

" I 'm too sharp to inquire for a left-handed hoe, Lige."

" That 's one of Tom Taylor's lies. I never done it."

" But you did try to deceive a poor girl, and you tried to ruin her reputation."

" Some gals is orful easy ruined, Zach."

" Come, come, boys. I like to have you spend your evenings with me, but you must not quarrel, or slander your neighbors."

" I would n't quarrel, if they 'd let me be, Uncle Henry; but they 're allers a pickin' at me, 'cause I make more money than they do."

And Elijah left the shop, slamming the door in a manner which clearly indicated his anger.

"I guess Lige is half right about Nellie Blunt."

"Yes, I believe he is. Blood will tell; and Jack Blunt has bad blood in his veins."

"She climbs trees like a Tom boy."

"And goes troutin' in short dresses."

"And combs her hair high up on her forrid."

"She puts perfumery on her handkercher."

"And they say she wears corsits."

"Wus than that; she danced with a stranger from the West'ard to the New Year's ball."

The conversation was interrupted by a young man, who had been a silent listener, taking his departure.

"Who is that young feller, Uncle Henry?"

"I don't know. He came in before the rest of you to leave his measure for a pair of slippers."

"He's a smart-lookin' chap."

"He's studyin' for a preacher."

"What makes you think so, Sam?"

"I see him git some books from Parson Green to-day."

"And I see him come out of Jack Blunt's, this afternoon."

"Did you notice how pale he was when he left?"

"Yes. There's too much terbacker smoke for him in here."

"It was not the tobacco smoke that made him sick."

"How do you know, Zach."

"The sickness caused by tobacco smoke does not pinch one's face as his was pinched. It is something worse than that."

Zach Brown was right. It was something worse than tobacco smoke. A poisoned arrow had entered the young man's heart, and almost stilled its pulsations. He loved Nellie Blunt.

"It couldn't be much worse than this terbacker smoke, Zach."

"Perhaps he was sorry to hear an innocent girl slandered."

"How do you know she is innercent?"

"How do you know she is guilty?"

"Appearances is agin her; and then she's Jack Blunt's daughter, and then Jack is bad blood."

"Her mother was an honest, intellectual, amiable woman."

"But they say girls takes mostly after their fathers."

"That is nonsense, Sam. I believe Nellie Blunt is an honest girl, and it is a shame for you boys to blacken her character. She has nothing in the world but her good name, and if you rob her of that, she will be poor indeed."

"We've only been tellin' what we've heered."

"You never heard a whisper against her character, save from the gossips that nightly assemble in this shop."

"That's right, Zach. Give 'em gowdy."

"Their conduct is shameful, Uncle Henry."

"So it is, my boy, and I hope you'll reform 'em."

"May be he's only tryin' to cover his own tracks, Uncle Henry."

"That's a cowardly insinuation, Sam Smith."

"Tut, tut, boys. No quarreling."

During the momentary lull that followed, Deacon Wells entered, and inquired for Elijah.

"Guess he went up to Jack Blunt's, Deacon."

"What does he want with Jack Blunt?"

"I kalkerlate his bizness is with Nellie."

"Git out with your nonsense. I squelched

that more 'n a month ago. Elijah can't marry that gal. She ain't got a cent in the world, and she would n't be no fit match for my boy."

"You 're right, Deacon. Elijah can't marry her."

"Now you 're talkin' sense, Ben. It would be a onsuitable match."

"Yes, sir. Too much lucifer about it."

" That 's the idee, Ben."

And Deacon Wells went home and told his wife that he "allers thought Ben Love was a smart boy."

"Wonder if the old skin-flint will vote for Jim at the polls?"

"You can bait your sweet life he won't, Ben. He 's never forgive him for ridin' old Charley down to Widow Brown's, and givin' her the money to pay her taxes. The Deacon had his heart sot on that Durham cow."

"If it had n't been for Jim Wells, Zach, your Aunt Elsie would have lost her cow."

"No. I saved up the money, and went down the same morning the old Deacon went to levy on the cow; but Jim had been there before me. I honor him for his kindness, and shall support him cordially, if we do differ in our political opinions. We need honest men in Congress."

" We need honest men everywhere, Zach."

" That's true, Uncle Henry; but we especially need them in Congress."

" You'll not get many of them there until the people quit sending the politicians."

" Jim Wells is not a politician."

" No. Jim Wells is an honest man. It's a pity to spoil such a man by sending him to Washington."

" Never fear. He will keep."

" Why can't they have things as they used to? We used to have honest men in office."

" Everything has changed. You don't make boots as you used to."

" Yes I do. I use nothing but hemlock tan, and I do my crimping by hand. I don't take kindly to these new-fangled ways."

" You're an exception, Uncle Henry."

" I wish we had a few exceptions in office."

" Lawyer Wells will be an ' exception '."

" So he will, if he gets there. The district is pretty close, and the Deacon's opposition may beat him."

“Success is often assured by the opposition of such men as Deacon Wells.”

“That’s true; but the Deacon has some influence in his church. They do n’t know him as well as we do, and then they’re a little put out with Jim for goin’ to hear Parson Green.”

“That cuts both ways, and Parson Green’s church is the largest.”

“I never thought of that. I must talk to the Parson about it.”

“I’ll guarantee that the Parson will support him.”

“I do n’t think the old Deacon has such a great sight of influence in his church, Uncle Henry.”

“Why not, Sam.”

“’Cause, father belongs, and he says Deacon Wells is a snide.”

“What’s a snide?”

“I do n’t know; but it ain’t anything good.”

“How do you know?”

“If it was, father would n’t say it of the old Deacon. He yank’d fifty dollars out of the old man on a hoss trade, and there’s no love atwixt ’em.”

" Is that where your father got that spavined alligator? "

" Yes.   He give the old Deacon fifty dollars to swop, and come home orful tickled.   He tho't he 'd got a big barg'in in that hoss."

" It is n't jest right for members of the same church to swop hosses.   They orter take in outsiders."

" There 's where Deacon Wells obeys the Scripter.   If a stranger comes along, he ' takes him in '."

" But he do n't stop at strangers.   He takes in his own church members."

" Well, the old fellow will find his match when he takes a twist with the devil."

" Do n't be too shure of that, Ben.   The devil has no bizness foolin' with Deacon Wells.   He 'd have a morgidge on the infernal regions afore he 'd been there a week."

" That won't work, Sam.   He could n't find nothin' to write it on."

" Yes he could.   He 'd take a sheet of brass from his face.   Then he 'd hunt up 'Squire Gray and have it foreclosed, get Jack Blunt and Tom Siddons to appraise h——ll at one-third of its value, buy it in at Sheriff's sale, and serve a notice on the devil to vacate."

"What would Elijah be doing all this time, Zach?"

"Oh, he'd be juking 'round, stealing the brimstone to start a match factory."

"S'posin' the old hypocrite should git to Heaven?"

"He wouldn't stay there. Men never spend much time with uncongenial associates."

"What would he do with the infernal regions, if he couldn't find Jack Blunt and Tom Siddons to appraise 'em for him?"

"He would be sure to find them. A man can't spend his life in the service of the devil, and then tack ship and sail into Heaven."

"You orter have been a preacher, Zach."

"There is plenty of material here to work upon."

"The harvist is ready for the sickle."

"Not until it ripens."

"Do you mean to insinerwate that we're green?"

"Not exactly green, Sam; but a man that will go to Tunk Lake to fish for togues, and freeze his feet on the ice while looking for holes that were cut the winter before, is only sun-baked."

"I did n't freeze my feet. I only frosted one of my toes."

"Was there any frost left, Sam?"

"My feet ain't so orful big, Ben."

"No; but they tell me an elephant can't pass them without blushing."

"My feet ain't nothin' compared with Lige Wellses."

"The deficiency in his head is made up in his feet. Your's ought not to be *quite* so large as his."

"He knows how to make money, Ben."

"That is all he knows. There is not a ten-year-old boy in Elton so ignoront as he. He went to school but a few months, and thought more of trading jack-knives than getting his lessons. All the father's avarice, and some of his low cunning, has been transmitted to Elijah, while he has inherited none of his mother's brains. He will never learn anything, except how to make a good bargain and cheat at cards."

"Did he inherit his fondness for cards from the Deacon?"

"They tell me the Deacon plays a rattling good game of draw poker when he gets away from home. Tom Taylor run across a man that had a little set-to with the old hypocrite at Bangor. Tom's friend was betting pretty lively on an ace-full, when the Deacon coolly took four queens from his coat pocket — as he reached for his tobacco — and raised him a hundred."

"Did the feller call him?"

"No. He raised him back two or three times, and finally called him and lost the money."

"How did he know the Deacon did n't get his hand honestly?"

"He counted the deck, and found it short?"

"Why did n't he make a fuss about it?"

"He had stolen his ace-full, and could n't do it with a good grace; and he thought he could get his money back by stealing the four aces, but the Deacon fought shy, and he could n't play it on him."

"Did Lige learn his card-playin' from the Deacon?"

"I do n't know. Jack Blunt says they play ten-cent ante in the barn loft, and Elijah rather beats the Deacon."

"Why do n't the Deacon's church haul him over the coals?"

"They do n't know it; and those who do know about it do n't wan't to tell and be hauled up as witnesses."

"That 's the way it goes, now-a-days. Rascals go free and prey upon the innocent, simply because honest men are too cowardly to prosecute them."

"Why do n't you prosecute him, Uncle Henry?"

"I have n't time."

"I presume that other honest men would offer the same excuse. The truth is, men who attend to their own business have but little time to meddle with the affairs of others."

"Nobody here has n't seen the old feller play cards, except Jack Blunt and Lige, and they would n't appear agin him."

"How do you know, Sam? Jack Blunt is a little out with the Deacon just now."

"I do n't care if he is. The Deacon owns him, and he darsent tell on him."

"What is Jack out with the Deacon about?"

"The Deacon promised to let him run the

mill on the Jones place, and backed down when Jack got ready to go."

"I s'pose he would n't object to Jack takin' double toll, but he did n't want him to steal it all."

"It would be a good thing if Jack would steal the mill, water privilege and all."

"Jack says the school-marm is goin' to try to git her part of the concern back."

"How does he know?"

"The Deacon sent him clear to Glenville to watch her, the other day, and he says she feed a lawyer."

"I hope she will succeed. It was a rascally piece of business throughout, and she and her brother were cheated out of ten thousand dollars by the old Deacon."

"And Jack Blunt helped to do it."

"Yes. He and Tom Siddons were the appraisers."

"A feller could take a quart of rum and pump it all out of Jack. I 've a notion to do it, and tell the mistress."

"You 'll have to take more 'n a quart, or Jack won't git any."

" Do n't worry about Jack not gittin' his share
of rum when there 's any 'round."

" Deacon Wells brought him a ten-gallon kag
when he come from Bangor, and it did n't last
him a fortni't."

" I 'll bait the Deacon put in four gallons of
rum and eight gallons of water. He ain't 'round
givin' away pure rum."

" How many gallons will a ten-gallon keg
hold, Sam ? "

" Ten gallons of rum, and twelve or thirteen
gallons of water. Water ain't so strong, you
know."

" Guess he 's got you there, Ben. A man can
hold more water than rum."

" Men are not kegs, 'though some of them do
hold a great deal of rum."

" How do these old guzzlers git their rum,
when the law is so hard agin it ? "

" Most of it is smuggled over from the Provinces. They say Deacon Wells has made a great
deal of money smuggling rum."

" Is there any deviltry that the Deacon ain't
into? He plays cards, cheats widows and
orphans, and smuggles rum. Seems to me

that orter be enough for a deacon in good standin'."

" Wan't the Deacon raised in the Provinces?"

" He was born in Nova Scotia, and was a hard ticket until he came here and joined church. "

"He wan't in earnest when he jined church, was he Ben?"

" No. It was only a blind, to conceal his real character."

" Well, I never knowed afore that the old cuss was a reg'lar blue-nose."

" You knowed he had an orful big nose, did n't you, Sam?"

" Yes; big enough for a railroad depo, but I did n't know 't was blue."

" What makes 'em call the Novey Skoshians ' blue-noses'?"

" 'Cause it gits so cold down there that a man's nose gits as blue as an indigo bag."

" If the people is all like the old Deacon, I should n't hanker arter 'em."

" How is it, Ben; you 've been there?"

" I liked the Provincials very much, Zach."

" Are they very stingy?"

"On the contrary; they are kind-hearted and liberal."

"They say they are agin free skules; and I do n't go a nine-pence on people that is down on free skules."

"That's a mistake, Sam. In Nova Scotia, where the free school system was introduced nine or ten years ago, it is heartily indorsed and warmly supported. In New Brunswick it has met with some opposition, but it has many friends there, and the opposition is dying out."

"Is it true that they put a jack-knife and a pine stick beside a Yankee's dinner plate, to keep him from whittling the table?"

"That's another mistake, Zach. They do n't whittle as much as we do; but they know how to treat people politely."

"And eat dry toast?"

"Yes; they eat a great deal of dry toast. It is found on the table at every meal."

"I should think they 'd get tired of it."

"Dry toast is to them what doughnuts are to us. A meal is not complete without it."

"Why do they eat so much more of it over

the line, in New Brunswick, than we do in Maine?"

"That is easily accounted for. The Provincial Government admits our low grades of flour free of duty. Much of the bread made from it is sour, and is not fit to eat until it is toasted; so dry toast is a necessity in the Provinces."

"Jim Wells cleared that little blue-nose, for stealin' money over to Sackarap, did n't he, Zach?"

"Yes. The little fellow was not guilty, but the Sackarapers would have sworn him squarely into the State prison if Jim had n't picked their evidence to pieces."

"None of them law lubbers has any bizness foolin' with Jim Wells. He kin wallop the best of 'em."

"Jess so. He 's sharper 'n a cambric needle."

"They say he did n't charge the little fellow a nine-pence for clearin' him."

"No. It was a 'labor of love' with him. The boy told his story, and Jim believed him innocent; and he will work harder to save a poor, innocent boy from unjust punishment than for a five hundred dollar fee."

"There ain't many lawyers will do it, Ben."

"Bessie Jones says there are as many good men among lawyers as in any of the professions."

"What does she know about lawyers?"

"She has been around a good deal, teaching school, and is acquainted with a great many lawyers. Her knowledge is not confined to teaching the young Eltonians to toe the mark and throw their shoulders back."

"You bait. She knows more 'n anybody."

"What does such a little chit as you know 'bout what the mistress knows?"

"She takes as much pains with us little uns as she does with you big lubbers, and she's jest as good as she can be. When I cut my finger, this mornin', she tied it up, and kissed me, and that's more 'n she'd do for you."

"You're right, Mountain Jack. He'd cut his finger to-morrow morning, if he thought the teacher would tie it up and kiss him."

"Of course he would; but she wouldn't kiss a great big mopsy like him."

"She kissed Ragged Bob the other day."

"Well, Ragged Bob's a little, pale-faced boy,. not much bigger 'n me."

"He could put you in his coat pocket, Jack. He's sixteen years old."

"No he couldn't. His coat pocket is all tore out. I give him an apple, this noon, and it went onto the ground, and Tom Seely grabbed it, and Nellie Blunt made him give it up."

"Yes; and Tom writ a verse on the blackboard about it."

"Can you repeat it?"

> "Nelly Blunt and Ragged Bob,
>   What a team they make;
> Bob gives Nell his chawin' gum,
>   And Nell gives Bob her cake."

"Yes. But the teacher made Tom ashamed, and made him rub it out before all the scholars."

"He wouldn't a rubbed it out if he wan't 'fraid of a lickin', Jack."

"Miss Jones is too good to lick anybody. She's the best mistress I ever went to."

"That's right, Mountain Jack. Stand up for the teacher."

"So I will, Uncle Henry, 'cause she sticks up for me."

"Come, boys, it's past nine o'clock, and I must close up."

And Uncle Henry went home, with his head filled with the good and bad things he had heard in the shop. One thought, however, was uppermost in his mind. He would see Parson Green, and talk with him about Jim Wells.

CHAPTER V.

AS chairman of the special committee, I have the honor, Mr. Wells, of informing you that you have received the nomination for Congressman of this District, and begging your acceptance."

"While I am not unmindful of the honor the convention has conferred upon me, my time is so fully occupied by my professional duties that I cannot canvass the District; and I have no desire to go to Congress. You know I am not a politician."

"That's why you were nominated, Mr. Wells. We are tired of the politicians, and want to try an honest man. You can be more useful in Congress than in practicing your profession."

"I am not willing to admit that; and if I accept the nomination, I shall have to take the stump and make a thorough canvass of the

District. This I cannot do. I will not stoop
to the disreputable practices that are considered
essential in a race for office."

"The people do not require that. You can
accept the nomination and discuss party issues
at the various county towns in the District?"

"I am willing to do that; and if that is all
the party will require at my hands, I will accept
the nomination."

"All right. You will surely be elected."

"I regard my election as one of the possibili-
ties, only. The District is very close, and my
opponent is an old politician; but defeat will
cause few regrets."

"You 'll beat him badly, Mr. Wells."

"Or accept the alternative, and be beaten."

It is not necessary to give the details of the
exciting political campaign that followed the
nomination of James Wells. He entered the
canvass reluctantly, and his first speech was not
remarkable; but the unjust criticism indulged in
by the press of the opposite party aroused him.
He discussed political questions in a manner
that clearly proved his familiarity with the history of his country. He swayed the masses by

his eloquence, and was triumphantly elected. "Was he elated by his success?" As well ask: "Is he human?"

———

A year has passed since Bessie Jones commenced her school at Elton. Lawyer Ainsworth is "making haste slowly," in the case of Bessie Jones *vs.* Hezekiah Wells, and the plaintiff is teaching the winter term, in the old red school house — the scene of Elijah Wells' pugilistic exploit. Honest John "sot her down" at Widow Love's, on his last trip, and her old pupils have welcomed her with a warmth that told how fondly she was loved.

"Ben tells me that you are going to Berwick, to-morrow, Mr. Wells."

"I have business there, and shall probably go to-morrow morning, Mrs. Love. Can I do anything for you there?"

"Nothing there; but I wish you would take Bessie Jones down with you. Her brother is not well, and she is worrying about him. He lives on the main road, about half way between here and Berwick. I thought you could take her home, and call for her on the way as you came back."

James Wells hesitated a moment. He knew how cruelly his father had wronged Bessie Jones, and he felt that to ask her to ride with him would place both in an embarrassing position.

"Has Miss Jones expressed a wish to go with me?"

"She do n't know you are going. I want to bring it about so that she won't know it was arranged beforehand. She's so afraid of troubling anybody."

" I am not acquainted with her, and she may object to riding with me."

"She knows you well by reputation, and if you call at our house on your way, and let me broach the subject, she will think it just happened so, and I know she will be delighted to go with you."

"You are always making things 'happen' for the benefit of others, Mrs. Love. I will call in the morning."

"Thank you."

"And I shall enjoin secrecy in regard to our plot."

"Should it be necessary for you to jump, I will let you know.   Be sure to jump out behind."—PAGE 99.

"All right. You will find that a woman can keep a secret as well as a Congressman."

The next morning the jingle of sleigh-bells attracted Bessie's attention, and she looked out of the window as a well-dressed gentleman drove a span of beautiful blacks up to the door."

"There is a caller, Mrs. Love."

"I declare! It's James Wells."

Did Bessie Jones want to meet him? That is a question she could not answer, satisfactorily, herself. His name was a household word. Mrs. Love and Ben were constantly singing his praises. She had learned to regard him as a hero, and her admiration was little less than reverence. But what would he think of her? Did he know about Elijah's offer of marriage? Had he a knowledge of her suit against his father? And, knowing, would he censure her? Before these questions were answered in her mind, Mrs. Love introduced James Wells. Both were slightly embarrassed, and — as usual with well-bred people — both were soon at ease. Were their first impressions favorable? Time will tell. Mrs. Love watched them with eager interest, and she was satisfied.

7

"Where are you going, this morning, Mr. Wells?"

"To Berwick."

"Oh, Bessie, here's a chance for you to go and see Harry. Mr. Wells passes right by your door."

"He may not desire to be troubled with a passenger."

"You are a very light 'trouble,' Miss Jones; and I have a good team."

"Can you oblige me without inconvenience to yourself?"

"It will afford me pleasure to take you."

"Thank you. I will be ready in ten minutes."

Before the allotted time expired, Bessie Jones entered the sitting room. She wore a blue merino dress, a brown beaver cloak, jaunty fur cap, with tippet and muff to match, and a pair of double-soled morocco boots. In short, she was dressed as a sensible woman would dress for a sleigh-ride in December. A single glance at her graceful form, classical features and sparkling, hazel eyes, convinced James Wells that she was beautiful, and he inwardly thanked Mrs. Love for "making things happen." As he was wrapping Bessie in the warm, fur robes, Mrs. Love came out with a stick of birch heated almost to burning.

"It will keep hot for an hour, and is long enough for both your feet."

Simultaneously they thanked Mrs. Love for her thoughtful care, James took the reins and the spirited horses started off in a gallop. Bessie realized that they were going at a fearful speed, and Mr. Wells could not control them.

"Do not fear, Miss Jones. I will keep them in the road."

"I am not afraid."

"Should it be necessary for you to jump, I will let you know. Be sure to jump out behind."

"I will."

A run of two miles brought them to a steep hill, and when they reached the top, they were easily controlled. James wisely applied the whip, and galloped them another mile.

"Were you not a little frightened, Miss Jones?"

"I hardly think I was frightened. I enjoyed

the bracing air, and the speed was exhilarating."

" Only a brave girl can enjoy a runaway."

" Does not entire freedom from responsibility
make one brave? You are driving, and I am
only a passenger."

" But you shared the danger."

" After your instructions about jumping out,
I had no fear."

" We are all right, now."

" Yes, sir; but you excited my curiosity by
whipping the horses when their speed was
checked, at the top of the hill."

" This is their first attempt to run with me,
and I do n't want them to know that I could not
control them. I think they will not try it again."

" I wish I could manage my pupils as easily."

" The young Eltonians are not so easily controlled as my horses. Judging from reports
about your school, your success in governing
it is encouraging. Some of your pupils — like
my blacks — will ' take the bit in their teeth,'
occasionally, but you very wisely make them
believe they are governed."

" Those who do not recognize parental authority are with difficulty governed in school, 'though nearly all my pupils are studious and obedient."

"You have far less trouble with them this winter than last?"

"Yes, sir. All my old pupils obey me, and I find their influence a great help in governing the new ones."

"After all, it is this great moral power that governs the world. Arbitrary laws cannot be enforced, because they are not backed by public sentiment. Even wholesome laws are not enforced in localities where public sentiment has been wrongly directed."

"What makes public sentiment, Mr. Wells?"

"Education. Public sentiment is cradled in the school-room. In places like Sackarap, for instance, a healthy public sentiment does not exist, because the people are very ignorant."

"Do you not sometimes find an unhealthy public sentiment in educated communities?"

"Rarely. It is true that educated people are occasionally misled by designing men; but, as a rule, they think for themselves, and are proof against evil influences."

"Are there not a great many educated criminals?"

"I think not. Many criminals possess a great deal of natural shrewdness and low cunning, but they are not educated."

"Yet you believe that many ignorant people are good?"

"Certainly. They were born good, and were reared by honest parents. I am a firm believer in hereditary transmission, Miss Jones."

"Does not the doctrine of hereditary transmission apply with equal force to criminals?"

"Undoubtedly; but education and association with educated people has a refining and elevating influence over them, and helps them to overcome a natural propensity to do wrong."

"Is it right for courts of justice to punish a criminal who inherits his evil propensities?"

"Courts are organized for the protection of the innocent, and cannot recognize hereditary transmission."

"Do they always protect the innocent?"

"I am sorry to say they do not. Judges and juries are sometimes tampered with, and the ends of justice subverted. This does not often occur; yet it is impossible to keep the ermine spotless. What do you imagine will be the fate of the hereditary criminals before the Highest Tribunal, Miss Jones?"

"I think that an All-wise God will consider their birth, and 'temper His justice with mercy.' I cannot believe that a man born and nurtured in crime, with uncontrollable propensities to evil, will receive no more consideration than one who, born of honest parents, and surrounded by good influences, forgets his early training and becomes a criminal in obedience to the dictates of his own will."

"I hope you are right. To punish them indiscriminately would not accord with our ideas of justice."

"Do you prosecute many criminals, Mr. Wells?"

"No. I never prosecute. I sometimes defend men charged with crime, when I consider them innocent."

"I presume innocent persons are rarely charged with crime."

"Not often. Honest men do not associate with criminals, and they seldom get into trouble ; but they are sometimes the victims of a conspiracy."

"I should think it would afford you pleasure to defend the innocent."

"It does; especially when I am sure that they are innocent before I undertake the defense. I am sometimes in doubt, and cannot work with a will."

"Do you consider it unprofessional to defend a guilty man?"

"It is not unprofessional; yet it is better that an attorney should believe his client innocent, if possible."

They rode on in silence for a few minutes, when Bessie pointed out a neat little cottage by the roadside.

"There is where we live."

"Does your brother live alone when you are teaching?"

"No, sir. Mrs. Deford lives in the house with us. She is very kind to Harry when I'm away."

"Mrs. Henry Deford?"

"Yes, sir."

"She is a rough diamond. She used to live in

Elton, and I remember her kindness to me when I was a little boy."

"You will come in and see your old friend?"

"Yes, Miss Jones. And I want to meet your brother, and learn his condition."

Bessie conducted Mr. Wells to her brother's room and introduced him. Harry was reserved, but he could not help admiring the fine-looking Congressman. Bessie had told her brother a great deal about James, gleaned from her conversations with Mrs. Love, and had thus disarmed much of his prejudice against the son of Deacon Wells. He knew that James left home because he could not indorse his father's evil ways, and he knew of his many acts of kindness; yet he looked upon Bessie's suit against the Deacon as a family quarrel, and he was slightly embarrassed when Bessie introduced him.

"Are you better, Harry?"

"Much better, sister, 'though I have not been really sick."

"Sick enough to want me, weren't you?"

"I want you always, Bessie; but I told John to tell you not to worry."

"He delivered your message; yet I learned from him that you looked paler than usual, and was suffering from the pain in your leg."

"The pain has left me, Bessie; and while I am glad to see you, I 'm almost sorry you came."

"We will differ on that point, Mr. Jones. I am *not* sorry she came."

"I have enjoyed the ride very much, and am going to enjoy my visit."

"Thank you. But I do n't want you to enjoy too much. If your brother will let me have my way, I will take him to Berwick, and have him back in two hours. I will then go to Melton, get through with my business, and call for you about six o'clock. This arrangement will give you half the day with your brother, and I am sure this bracing air will benefit him."

Harry hesitated. A glance at Bessie's face told him plainly that she wanted him to go, and he accepted the invitation.

"While you are getting ready, I will step in and see Mrs. Deford."

———

"Good morning, Mrs. Deford."

" Well, I declare! You 've got the disadvantage of me. I believe I do n't know you."

" Do n't you remember the boy that helped Isaac shear your gray sheep?"

James showed the scar on his wrist that the kind-hearted old woman had tied up twenty years ago.

" I declare to grashus! Be you little Jimmy Wells?"

"Jimmy Wells, but no longer 'little.' I weigh a hundred and eighty pounds."

" Who 'd a thought you 'd been a great big boy so soon?"

" That was twenty years ago, Mrs. Deford."

" So 't was; and that gash you got with the sheep shears still sticks by you?"

" Yes, ma'am. I keep it to remember you and Isaac by."

" What a time you and Ike *did* have shearin' that old gray sheep, to be shure."

" That old gray sheep was a tough customer, Aunty."

" So he was.. I biled one of his hind quarters a hull day, and then 't was so tough I had to bake it. Ike sold the fore quarters, and give the other hind quarter to our minister. Ike and the minister was allers havin' tilts with each other, you know. A wile after'ards, Ike asked the minister how he liked his lamb, and the minister told him it was tender compared to the heart of a man that would kill a old, gray-headed sheep, sell the pelt, and give the sole leather to the minister. He asked Ike why he did n't keep the mutton, and have his boots half-soled with it. Ike told him he had whole-sold a minister, and that was better 'n half-solin' his boots. And so they had it; but the minister was jest as good as he could be, if he wan't sharp enough for Ike."

"Yes, Aunty; Elder Cole was a good man."

"So he was. He was always sound in doctrin' if he wan't so very flowery; and I knit him a pair of good, warm stockins out of that gray wool, and run 'em, heel and toe; and do n't you think, I 've got stockins in the house, this minit, that was knit from that identical sheep, and a ball of yarn besides, and if ever you git marrid I 'll knit your fust baby a pair of stockins with it. Maybe I can't size 'em jest right, for its a long time sense I 've knit a stockin' for a baby;

but I 'll make 'em big enough so it can grow to 'em.''

"Thank you. I think I shall not need them for several years."

"They say you 've gone to Congress, and maybe you 'll find somebody there that 'll take your eye."

"I was elected last fall, but I 've not been to Washington yet. I shall probably go next week."

"I allers felt that you 'd be one of the elect. Do n't let them high-steppin' chaps spile you, Jimmy. They say they 're a bad set."

"I 'll look out for them, Aunty. Good bye."

"Good bye, Jimmy. Remember, I 'm goin' to knit them stockins for your fust baby."

"I will remember."

James carefully tucked the warm robes about Harry's feet, bade Bessie good bye, and started for Berwick. The blacks did not attempt to run, and Bessie was relieved from her anxiety as they started off in a gentle trot. She knew that Harry could not "jump out behind."

Under the exhilarating influence of the bracing air and pleasant ride, Harry was happy and communicative. James soon discovered that his mind was stored with useful knowledge, and he was surprised to learn how much he knew of the great world in which he mingled so little. They discussed politics, theology, and metaphysics. On these subjects Harry evinced a thorough knowledge, the result of careful research and deep thought. James was delighted. He directed the conversation from one subject to another with a nice discernment, that would have done credit to an accomplished diplomat, and was pleased to learn that Bessie and Harry were familiar with the French, German, Latin, and Greek languages.

" How does Bessie find time to prosecute her studies and teach school?"

"She studies very hard during her three-months' vacation, and devotes a portion of her evenings to the languages while teaching."

" That is the pursuit of knowledge under difficulties."

" Yes, sir. 'Greek Without a Master' will do

to talk about, but it is difficult to master Greek,
'though Bessie will do it. She is very anxious
to become proficient in the languages."

"Is she studying with a view to teaching the
languages?"

"Yes, sir. She thinks that teaching will be
her life-work."

"It is a hard life, Harry."

"So it is; but Bessie says it has its compensations."

That moment James Wells resolved that, if he
could prevent it, Bessie Jones should not wear her
life out in teaching Latin and Greek. Visions
of a select school, with a limited number of
pupils, floated through his mind, and he fondly
hoped that he might need "them stockins"
before many years rolled around.

He was detained but a short time in Berwick,
and he landed Harry at his home before twelve.
A happy party partook of the meal that Bessie
had prepared. The ride sharpened their appe-
tites, and the viands, prepared with skill and
spiced by interesting conversation, disappeared
with a rapidity that would have gladdened the
heart of an experienced cook. At half past one

o'clock James started for Melton.   His business was soon disposed of, but he did not wish to return at once.   The moon would shine in the evening, and by starting from Melton at five o'clock he would reach Mrs. Love's before nine. This would give the orphans another hour together, and he felt that every moment was precious to them.   He strolled into a book store and whiled away the hour in examining the latest publications.   Selecting three — one for himself, and one each for Bessie and Harry — he started for home, anticipating a pleasant talk with Bessie.   When he reached her, he learned that she and Harry were waiting for him to sup with them, and he gladly accepted the cordial invitation.   After supper he presented the books, which were thankfully received.   This led to a discussion of the merits of prominent authors, and all were unmindful of the flight of time until the clock struck nine.   James was surprised at the lateness of the hour, and was about to apologize, when it occurred to him that an apology was not required.   He suggested that Mrs. Love would grow weary of waiting for them, and proposed to start at once.   Harry urged them to stay, James regretted that they could not remain, and Bessie was silent, feeling that she was "only a passenger."

As James and Bessie bade Harry good night, Mrs. Deford came to the door:

"Do n't forgit to let me know when you want them baby stockins, Jimmy."

"I will not forget, Mrs. Deford. Good bye."

"Good bye. And keep your eyes peeled for them high-steppers in Congress. The papers say they 're an ungodly set, and do nothin' but eat biled oysters and drink shampain. Do n't let 'em spile you, Jimmy."

"I 'll give them a wide berth, Aunty."

"Jess so. Let 'em sleep on the floor, if they will. It 's good enough for 'em."

"Mrs. Deford's opinion of Congressmen is not flattering, Mr. Wells."

"No, ma'am; but it may not be incorrect."

"I hope you will find them better than her picture."

"I trust they are not much worse than other men; yet, judging from reports, they spend too much time at the festive board. I have not an exalted opinion of Washington society, 'though there are, doubtless, many good men in Congress."

"When do you go?"

"The last of next week."

"So soon?"

"Yes, ma'am. I want to reach Washington two or three days before the opening."

Why did Bessie say "So soon?" Why should the time of Mr. Wells' departure interest her? Did she already love the man whom she had, that morning, almost feared to meet?

"How long will you remain?"

"Until next summer."

"Will it not interfere with your professional duties?"

"Somewhat; but I regret, more than all, that I cannot visit Augusta, this winter, in the interest of the Educational bill."

"I hope that bill will be adopted by the Legislature. It will reform our present system; but it seems to me that there is an important feature omitted."

"What is that?"

"Uniformity in our text books."

"Is it practicable?"

"I think so. At present too much is left to the discretion of the teacher. It is not uncommon to find pupils well advanced in algebra and totally ignorant of grammar and rhetoric, while in many schools physiology is not even introduced."

"You are right, Miss Jones, and I thank you for the suggestion. I shall write to the chairman of the committee, and will endeavor to have your idea ingrafted in the bill. New England educators have an inherent fondness for mathematics, and many of them lose sight of other important branches, in their anxiety to make their pupils proficient in algebra."

"I don't think the inborn veneration for mathematics is confined to New England educators, Mr. Wells. It exists in the West and South."

"Many of the educators in the West and South are Yankees, Miss Jones."

"True; but in the West, especially, many of the teachers are natives, and they still cling to mathematics with all the tenacity of a New England pedagogue."

"It is not taught in the West, as in New

England, at the expense of many other useful branches."

"Not to the same extent, perhaps; but it is permitted to encroach upon important studies in the West, as elsewhere. While it should not be neglected, it is certainly unwise to require a pupil to spend three-fourths of the time devoted to study in attempting to master mathematics."

"What, in your opinion, is the most important study, Miss Jones?"

"I should hesitate in giving precedence to any particular branch, Mr. Wells; but I think that if time spent in working out the difficult and impractical problems of higher mathematics, and locating obscure rivers in Asia, were devoted to grammar, rhetoric, physiology, and the science of government, it would be infinitely better for the pupil."

"Does not a thorough knowledge of mathematics make a good foundation for an education?"

"Yes, sir; but as taught under our system, it is much like preparing a granite foundation for a cob house."

"With woman's tact, you have settled the question by comparison."

"Women do not think as much as men, and are apt to reason by comparison."

"You have, evidently, thought much about education."

"Because it is my business. While my thoughts are circumscribed, yours are not confined to the law."

"The wide range of our discussion to-day proves that your thoughts are not circumscribed."

"You forget that my part of the discussion was confined to asking questions."

"By no means. You have taught me several important lessons."

"Then you are my first advanced pupil. Seriously, I am of the opinion that women are not bold thinkers. Men originate and women copy. We rarely invent anything, and seldom succeed in a field that requires deep thought and originality, while as copyists we can successfully contest the honors with the sterner sex."

"You have not had equal opportunities."

"We have not improved the opportunities that are given us. Take, for instance, the science of music. Woman can perform the most difficult productions with a clearness of conception, and fineness of touch, that proves her execution faultless, yet she has not risen to eminence as a composer. You will concede that, in this department, more attention is paid to the education of women than men?"

"And if I do, how will you account for woman's failure?"

"There are several reasons why she does not succeed. She is not a free thinker, and she is hampered by petty cares."

"All women are not 'hampered by petty cares,' Miss Jones."

"Some are comparatively free, yet none absolutely untrammeled. Much of woman's time is spent in ornamenting her wardrobe and making pastry."

"Then you do not believe in making pastry?"

"I think more potatoes and less pastry would be better for both sexes."

"And you advocate dress reform?"

"I believe in dress reform, 'though I do not advocate it. So much has been said on the subject, that it is already hackneyed, and the discussion is barren of good results."

" All reforms are brought about by discussion. I think the intelligent women of America will finally inaugurate a reform in dress."

" The ' intelligent women of America' yield implicit obedience to the dictates of Fashion, Mr. Wells, and I have little hope of reform. Man would not suffer so much inconvenience, but woman dares not assert her independence. And, then, the subject of dress reform has been discussed in connection with the suffrage question until both are odious in the minds of many sensible women."

" Then you do not believe in woman's rights?"

" Not as you construe the term. I believe that when a woman does her work equally as well as a man, she should receive a man's wages. I believe that a married woman should have the right to make contracts and hold property independent of her husband; but I cannot see how she will be benefited by suffrage. Certainly not by agitating the muddy waters of party politics."

" Give woman the right of suffrage, and will she not bring about the reforms you mention?"

" I think not. Men will lead and women will

follow. Nine-tenths of the married women will vote with their husbands, and the others will not go to the polls. The time spent in discussing the suffrage question could be more profitably spent in advocating necessary reforms. Men will deal justly with us when they learn our real needs. They are simply blinded by the dust of the suffrage question."

"I think there are many matters in which woman should feel a deeper interest than in the question of suffrage. Our laws relating to the rights of married women are unjust and oppressive. In case of the husband's death, she is the natural, but not the lawful, guardian of her own children, while the law makes the father the guardian of his children whether the mother be living or dead. There are many other cases of unjust discrimination between husbands and wives. Many of the Western States are far in advance of us in righting these matters."

"Yes, sir. Our people are eminently conservative, and very slow to adopt even needed reforms."

The discussion was continued until they reached Mrs. Love's. The weather had moderated, the moon was shining brightly, and James intentionally protracted the ride.

"Have you been sitting up for us, Mrs. Love?"

"Not long. It is so pleasant that I did n't expect you home early. Come in and get a lunch, Mr. Wells. I have a cup of hot tea, some warm muffins, and a plate of doughnuts, for you and Bessie."

James did not try to resist the temptation to spend another hour with Bessie. Like a sensible man, he tied his horses and went in.

"Did you enjoy your ride, Bessie?"

"Very much; and I am under obligations to you for suggesting to Mr. Wells that I wanted to go."

"How is Harry?"

"Much better, thank you. He went to Berwick with Mr. Wells, and the ride did him so much good."

"Then we were both benefited, Miss Jones. I enjoyed his company exceedingly."

"I am so glad you all had a good time. Now give me your wraps, and see if you can enjoy my muffins."

"I can't answer for Miss Jones; but you know that I always enjoy them, Mrs. Love, and I imagine they will be especially enjoyable to-night."

"I hope so; for I feel like having a good chat with you. You call so seldom, lately, Mr. Wells."

"I have been very busy, Mrs. Love. I shall call again before I leave home."

"You used to call every week."

"I had plenty of leisure then. Clients were not numerous; and I was glad to borrow a little sunshine from you."

"You have returned it with interest."

"Thank you."

The trio "enjoyed the muffins" and the tea. There is an indescribable exhilaration in a cup of tea, that is not confined to the fair sex. The "lords of creation" may disclaim and call it woman's beverage, but they feel its potent influence, and relish its trimmings of gossip. The little party that gathered around Mrs. Love's bright fire-place took tea without trimmings, but the stream of interesting conversation flowed for an hour without interruption, when

James reluctantly bade the jolly hostess and the happy schoolma'am good night.

During the next week James had business with Mrs. Love almost every evening. It was dispatched with remarkable rapidity, and he devoted most of the time to Bessie. On Monday evening she gave directions about the collection of a small note. On Tuesday, Wednesday, and Thursday evenings he came for additional instructions. There was a merry twinkle in the widow's eyes as she admitted him on Thursday evening. She answered his unimportant question about "that note," plead a severe headache, and asked to be excused. Her request was granted with seeming reluctance. If you are a genuine Yankee, dear reader, you "guess" it was only seeming.

"Good bye, Bessie. Shall I write to you?"

"It will afford me pleasure to hear from you often."

CHAPTER VI.

THE FORGERY.

HELLO, JACK; wouldn't you like to be a Justice of the Peace?"

"I don't know. Is there any money in it?"

"Some money, and lots of onner."

"How 'll I git the office, Deacon?"

"I 'll git 'Squire Gray to write to the Govner and git you appinted. 'Squire Blunt will sound kind o' good."

"What does the Govner care about 'Squire Gray?"

"'Squire Gray helped him in the nominashun, and 't ain't very hard to git a Justice appinted if the fust person that moves in it has inflooence, and that 's me."

"Well, I ain't a carin', Deacon; but there's 'Squire Shaw don't make enough out o' the office to buy salt for his porridge."

"You'll make more nor him. I've got a. twenty-five-dollar job for you to begin with, and I'll give you lots o' notes to sue on."

"All right. Bring along your office. I'll take it."

"I'll go and see 'Squire Gray, and git you appinted."

"What is that little job you spoke of, Deacon?"

"Time enough to tell you about that when you're a actin' Justice, Jack. I ain't noted for talkin' too much, like some people I know of."

"Air you alludin' to me, Deacon?"

"If the shoe fits you, you can wear it a little wile, Jack; but we won't quarrel about that. Let by-gones be by-gones; but look out for by-gones in the futer."

"I can keep my tongue still when its ankered with silver."

"But it takes too heavy a anker, Jack. You've got more 'n a hundred dollars out o' me, and if there's anybody what orter keep his tongue atween his teeth, it's Jack Blunt."

"And I've made you more 'n a thousand dollars, Deacon."

"There's where you're rattled. I made all my own money accordin' to law, as everybody knows."

"I guess you made some of it accordin' to Jack Blunt and Tom Siddons. Don't you remember that Jones bizness?"

"The less you say about that Jones bizness the better you'll be off, Jack. Apprisin' a place for one-third it's wuth is a penitenshary offense, and you'd better keep mum."

"If I was in State's prison, where would you be, Deacon?"

"In Elton, I s'pose... They can't tetch me for buyin' property at the apprisement."

"If they found out that you paid me and Tom Siddons fifty dollars for apprisin' of it, I guess they'd take you along with us."

"No they wouldn't, Jack. I've perceeded accordin' to law, as I allers do; but there's no use talkin' about that. Keep mum, and stick to the goose that lays the golden aig."

"I will; but I want a little of the aig once in a wile."

"You shall have it, Jack."

"Elijah, put the saddle on old Charley for me. I 'm goin' down to 'Squire Gray's."

"What 's in the wind now, father?"

"I want him to git Jack Blunt appinted Justice of the Peace."

"Why do n't you git a holler fence pole appinted?"

"No nonsense, Elijah. Jack Blunt is the makin' of a good 'Squire."

"He do n't know nothin' about law."

"'Squires do n't need to."

"Jack Blunt ain't overly onest."

"If he was, I would n't want him appinted, Elijah."

"Oh, ho! There 's somethin' brewin', father. Can't ye tell a feller?"

"Not jest yet. I 'll show you them four aces bimeby."

The Deacon interviewed Esquire Gray, and a petition for the appointment of Jack Blunt was sent to the Governor. The Esquire's nerves were steady when he wrote: "Mr. Blunt possesses, in an eminent degree, the Jeffersonian qualifications." The Governor brought the matter up in Council, vouched for Jack Blunt, and in due time his commission was forwarded. A shrewd politician never kicks down the ladder by which he ascends, and Esquire Gray is one of the rounds of the Governor's ladder.

———

"Patience, go up stairs. Me and Elijah has a little privacy, and wimmin has no bizness 'round when there's privacy goin' on."

Patience Wells left the room with a heavy heart. She knew that "little privacy" meant fraud, and she could not prevent it.

"Elijah, have you got that deed you writ out for Bessie Jones to sign?"

"Yes, sir. It's on the top shelf in the parler cubberd."

"Jack Blunt has got his appintment, and we'll take it up to his house, sign Bessie's name to it, and git Jack to acknolige it."

"Won't we git into a scrape?"

"No, indeed. There'll be Jack's acknoligment to prove she signed it herself; don't you see?"

"Oh, yes. You've got them four aces, shure enough.'

" I'll sign it myself.   I can write smallish, like a woman."
— Page 130.

"I allers hold 'em when they 're needful, Elijah."

"You do; shure 's you 're born."

"And there 's nobody knows no better how to play 'em than your old father, Elijah."

"You can beat the man that made 'em, father."

———

"Now, Jack, send that gal of yourn out o' the house. We 're on bizness."

"Nellie is busy in the kitchen, Deacon, and she won't be in here."

"Gals is allers peekin' 'round, 'Squire Blunt, and you 'd better send her to the neighbors."

"She won't send wuth a cent, Deacon, and we 'll go up stairs and lock the door. She 'll think somethin 's in the wind if we send her away."

"Gals orter be trained up to mind, Jack; but if it 's all safe up stairs, we 'll go. Bring a pen and ink along."

"All right."

The three villains went up to the little chamber. Jack locked the door, and the Deacon told him what he expected him to do. He assented, and Elijah produced the deed.

"Now sign Bessie Joneses name to it, Elijah."

"That won't do, Deacon. It must be a different hand-writin' from the deed."

"That's so, Jack. You will have to sign it."

"That won't do nuther. My writin' will be in the acknoligment."

"I will sign it myself. I can write smallish, like a woman."

Deacon Wells signed Bessie's name to the deed. Jack Blunt wrote the acknowledgment, and the old Deacon placed the instrument in his side pocket.

"Now we've got 'er. Less go home, Elijah."

"Hold on, Deacon. You're forgittin' that twenty-five dollars, and I'm for gittin' it."

"You're rather hard on me, Jack. I kalkerlate fifteen dollars is a big price; don't you, Elijah?"

"You orter to do that little writin' for ten, Jack, and that is a orful price."

"Your father promised me twenty-five dollars, Lige, and it's dirt cheap at that. Look at the resk I 'm runnin' by that little acknolig-ment."

" We run jest as much risk, and do n't git a cent for it."

" Do n't, hey! What is that little dockeyment wuth to you?"

" 'T ain't wuth twenty-five dollars, Jack; but here 's your money. If ever this comes up in court you 'll have to swear that Bessie Jones signed the deed herself."

" But s'posin' I do n't swear to that, then what?"

" You 'll be tried for forgin', and sent to the penitenshary; that 's all."

" When I go to the penitenshary for that little writin' there 'll be a church in Elton lookin' 'round for a new deacon. Mind that."

" What 'll they want of a new deacon?"

" The old 'un will be learnin' a trade with me."

" If you ain't a born fool, and afeared to swear, you won't go to the penitenshary, Jack."

" Come, father, less go home. You need n't be afeared of Jack. He 'll swear all right."

On their way home, Deacon Wells and his son discussed Jack Blunt's character.

"S'posin' Jack should git ugly, father, he'd have us in a short row?"

"He'll not git ugly, Elijah. I know too much agin him."

———

"Here's a letter from 'Squire Gray, Elijah. He says the case of Bessie Jones agin Hezekiah Wells is sot for day after to-morrer. We will have to go to court. Won't they be took back when they see that deed? Ketch a weesil asleep, will ye?"

"We've got 'em, father."

"Yes; and we'll hold 'em, Elijah."

"Shure's you're born."

At the appointed time the case was called and the trial commenced. Lawyer Ainsworth proved, without difficulty, that no notice was served on his client, and moved to set the sale aside, so far as it affected the rights of Bessie Jones.

Esquire Gray arose, with the air of a man who feels that he can annihilate his opponent:

"May it please the Court, I have an objection to interpose."

"State your objection."

"The sale is good so far as the interest of Harry Jones is concerned, and we will save the expense of another trial by introducing a quit-claim deed for Bessie's interest in her father's place. Here is the deed, your Honor."

" Pass it to Mr. Ainsworth."

The practiced eye of Mr. Ainsworth detected the forgery at once. The signature was coarse, and evidently the work of a man's hand. It was written "Besse" Jones, and he unhesitatingly pronounced it a forgery.

Esquire Gray proposed to prove the execution of the deed, and called Deacon Wells to the witness stand. After the usual preliminary questions, he asked:

" Deacon Wells, did you ever see this deed before? "

" Ever see it afore? To be shure I have. I 've carried it in my pocket for nearly a year."

" Was it executed by the plaintiff, Bessie Jones? "

" No, sir. It was executed by my Elijah, and signed by Bessie Jones afore 'Squire Blunt. The deed shows for itself."

“Then it was written by your son, Elijah?”

“Yes, sir; Elijah writ it and Bessie signed it.”

“Did you see her sign it?”

“Yes, sir.”

“Where did she sign it?”

“Afore ’Squire Blunt, in the little chamber, up stairs.”

“What was the consideration?”

“In considerashun of her duty, I s’pose.”

“But what did you pay her for her interest in the property?”

“Elijah paid her; but I do n’t consider as she had an intrust in it.”

“How much did he pay her?”

“He give her a five-dollar dress; and that was more ’n ’t was wuth.”

“Where did he give her the dress?”

“To ’Squire Blunt’s, the mornin’ she signed the deed.”

“Did any one besides you and ’Squire Blunt see her sign the deed?”

“Yes, sir.   Elijah see her.   He ’s over to Jim Hickey’s bakin’ shop, and he ’ll come and swear to it.”

“You can take the witness, Mr. Ainsworth.”

Mr. Ainsworth talked a moment with Bessie, and commenced the cross-examination:

"You are very sure that you saw Bessie Jones sign this deed?"

"Yes, sir; as shure's my name's Hezekiah Wells."

"What time in the afternoon did she sign it?"

"About one o'clock; jest afore her skule called."

"And she signed it in presence of 'Squire Blunt and Elijah?"

"Yes, sir. 'Squire Blunt, Elijah and me was present."

"Do you know 'Squire Blunt to be a regularly commissioned Justice of the Peace?"

"I orter know it. I was the fust man that moved in gittin' him appinted."

"Then he was appointed by your request?"

"Yes, sir. Mine and 'Squire Gray's."

"Can you spell Bessie Jones' name?"

"I guess so. Anybody that knows anything about spellin' can do that."

"You may spell it, if you please, Deacon."

"B-e-s Bes s-e se, Besse, J-o-n-e-s Jones, Besse Jones."

"That will do, Deacon."

Deacon Wells left the stand with a self-satisfied air, failing to notice the broad grin that came so near demoralizing the Bench and Bar. Elijah Wells was called, and Esquire Gray proceeded with his "proof."

"Elijah, did you ever see this instrument before?"

"What! that deed?"

"Yes, sir."

"Guess I have, 'Squire. I writ it."

"Who signed it?"

"Bessie Jones."

"Where?"

"At Widow Love's."

"Was Mrs. Love present?"

"No, sir. She runs 'round to the neighbors a good deal."

"What was the consideration?"

"The what?"

"What did you pay her for signing the deed?"

"I didn't pay her nothin' for signin' the deed. I give her twenty-five dollars for her quit-claim to her intrust in the place that already belonged to dad."

"Were you present when she signed the deed?"

"To be shure I were."

"And twenty-five dollars was the consideration?"

"I s'pose that's what you call it. I know I give her the money."

"You can take the witness, Mr. Ainsworth."

"Your name is Elijah Wells?"

"Jess so."

"You are the son of Deacon Hezekiah Wells?"

"So they say."

"And you wrote that deed?"

"Yes, sir."

"Who asked you to write it?"

"Dad."

"Where did you get the description of the land?"

"I took the deed the Sheriff give dad, and writ it jest like it."

"You say you were present when the deed was signed?"

"Yes, sir."

"And it was signed at Mrs. Love's?"

" Yes, sir."

" Was your father present? "

" No, sir."

" Was 'Squire Blunt there? "

" No, sir. Bessie went afore Jack Blunt to acknolige the deed, but he wan't there when she signed it."

" When was it signed? "

" I do n't jest remember. Somethin' like two weeks ago. 'T was the day Jack Blunt got his appintment."

" How do you know it was on that day? "

" 'Cause dad told me Jack had jest got his papers, and we 'd go up and sign the deed."

" Go up to Jack's house and sign the deed? "

" No, sir. Go and git it acknoliged."

" And you went up? "

" Yes, sir."

" Who did you find at 'Squire Blunt's? "

" Nobody but Jack. Nellie was in the kitchen."

" Who went with you? "

" Dad."

" Then you and your father were the only persons present when the deed was acknowledged? "

"Jess so."

"Where was Bessie Jones?"

"Teechin' skule, I s'pose."

"Who paid 'Squire Blunt for taking the acknowledgment?"

"Dad paid him twenty-five dollars for it. It was a orful price, and I told Jack so."

"Did your father grumble at the price?"

"He sort o' tried to git Jack to come down, but he did n't come down wuth a cent."

"What reason did he give for charging such an exorbitant price for taking an acknowledgment?"

"There was nothin' said about that kind of a price. Jack claimed that dad promised him twenty-five dollars, and he stuck and hung for it like a hungry cat in butcherin' time."

"Do you know what induced your father to promise such a sum?"

"No, sir. I could got it done for ten if I 'd made the bargin."

"You like to make a good bargain, do you not, Elijah?"

"Yes, sir. But I hain't such a hankerin' that way as some folks."

"Yet you bought Bessie Jones' interest in the old homestead very low?"

"Yes, sir; but that was because dad owned it afore. I do n't count that a sharp bargin, but I often make 'em buyin' yearlin's and clam priv-'leges."

"That will do, Elijah. You may stand aside."

"Can I set down, if I want to?"

"Certainly."

Bessie Jones was called, and stated that she never conveyed her interest in the old home-stead. Esquire Gray knew that she told the truth, and he did not cross-examine her. Dea-con Wells wanted Jack Blunt to "take a swear at the case," but Jack could not be found. The sale was set aside, and Bessie Jones was declared the owner of the undivided one-half of the homestead in fee simple.

Deacon Wells started home in an ill humor. He had played a desperate game, and lost. He did not think of the consequences of his crime. He had lost five thousand dollars.

"Well, father, that's the fust time I ever knowed four aces beat."

" You conterdicted my evidence, Elijah, and Jack Blunt wan't there to swear."

" How did I know what you was goin' to swear to, father?"

" If you'd been in the court room instead of munchin' pies at Jim Hickey's, you'd a knowed how to swear."

" I was hungry, and I had to have somethin' to eat."

" If you'd put a doughnut in your pocket, instead of spendin' your money at Jim Hickey's, you'd be better off. I'll have to sell my bank stock to pay Bessie Jones."

" What will you have to pay her, father?"

" 'Squire Gray thinks he can git 'round her and git a deed for three thousand dollars; but that is a good deal of money, Elijah, and we'll have to cut close to save it up."

" The mill will make it in two years. It's clearin' more 'n fifteen hundred a year."

" Three thousand dollars is a big pile. I'll ask him to try her on two."

———

" Here's a deed for your undivided half of the

old place, Miss Jones. I have put the sum of three thousand dollars as the consideration. That sum 'will be clear. The sale will stand as it was originally made; that is, the Deacon will have no recourse on you for the recovery of a part of the original purchase money, which went to pay your father's debts. The price is what I consider fair, under the circumstances, and if it suits you, you may sign the deed."

"I want to deal justly with Deacon Wells, notwithstanding his attempt to defraud me; but I don't know what I ought to ask for my interest in the property. I shall leave the matter with Mr. Ainsworth."

"You'd better fix the price yourself, Miss Jones. Some lawyers don't always do the best thing for their clients."

"I have confidence in Mr. Ainsworth, and I am sure he will be just to all parties concerned."

Esquire Gray left Bessie Jones feeling that he was already foiled. He could not persuade Mr. Ainsworth to take a penny less than the full value of the property; but he must try, for his client expected it. He took the morning stage for Glenville.

"How do you do, Mr. Ainsworth? Are you very busy to-day?"

"Very well, and not too busy to smoke with you. Sit down."

"I came to talk with you about that Jones property. Bessie says you are authorized to dispose of her interest."

"Yes, sir. By the way, 'Squire, that was a very foolish piece of business, forging that deed. It was a bungling job."

"Do you intend to prosecute him for it?"

"No. I have too much respect for James to assist in prosecuting his father; but the Grand Jury will probably indict him."

"I hope the matter will be dropped."

"They will hardly pass by such an offense. It is in everybody's mouth. But what proposition do you make about the property?"

"I thought about three thousand dollars would be a fair price for it, considering all the circumstances. I suppose Bessie would be held for one-half her father's debts, and three thousand dollars would be about right for a quit-claim deed."

"Her father's debts are paid. If Deacon

Wells wants to convey his half of the property, we will refund the purchase money with interest, and give him a thousand dollars bonus. I have been offered three thousand dollars for one-half the hemlock bark."

"What is your lowest price for Bessie's interest?"

"Eight thousand dollars."

"You can't find a purchaser at that price."

"Can't I? I shall sell it for that sum before next Saturday evening. Mark that."

"Good day, Mr. Ainsworth. I will state your proposition to my client."

"Good day, 'Squire. Tell him to hurry up, if he wants the place."

"I will."

"Good morning, Deacon."

"How do do, 'Squire?"

"I went to see Bessie Jones, and she referred me to Mr. Ainsworth. I went to Glenville to see him, and he asks eight thousand dollars for Bessie's interest."

"E-i-g-h-t t-h-o-u-s-a-n-d d-o-l-l-a-r-s!"

" Yes, sir.   That is his lowest price."

" He 'll wait a long wile for a buyer, 'Squire."

" He says he will sell it before next Saturday night."

" Who 'll pay that much for it ? "

" I do n't know; but he has his eye on a purchaser.   He has been offered three thousand dollars for Bessie's share of the hemlock bark."

" Three thousand dollars for the bark ? "

" Yes, sir."

" 'Squire Gray, Ainsworth is lyin' to you."

" So he is, father.   There 's nobody that 'ud be fool enough to pay three thousand dollars for all the hemlock bark in Maine."

" Oh, yes, Elijah.   The Shaws paid ten thousand dollars for the hemlock bark on the Belt land."

" Do you believe Ainsworth was tellin' you the truth, 'Squire ? "

" Yes, I do, Deacon.   He says he will pay your money back, with interest, and a thousand dollars bonus, if you 'll convey your half of the place."

" Take him up, father."

" Do n't gallup when you 're goin' down hill,

10

Elijah. The mill pays over fifteen hundred a
year."

"Perhaps you had better go and see Mr. Ainsworth yourself, Deacon?"

"So I will. I 'll go to-morrer."

The Deacon went to Glenville the next morning, sold his bank stock, and bought Bessie's
interest from Mr. Ainsworth for the price
named, after trying for an hour to get it for less.

"Now, Mr. Ainsworth, 'Squire Gray says you
know a man that wants the hemlock bark on the
place?"

"Yes, sir."

"What 'll he give for it?"

"Six thousand dollars."

"Send him along, and I 'll give you a five-
dollar bill."

"I can't work so cheap as that, Deacon. I
wan't five per cent. for selling it."

"How much will that be?"

"Three hundred dollars."

"Three hundred dollars for sellin' a little hemlock bark?"

"Six thousand dollars is not a small sum for
bark."

"I guess I'll keep the bark awile, Mr. Ainsworth."

"All right. Let me know when you conclude to sell it."

"Maybe I will."

Deacon Wells spent a week in riding about the country, inquiring of every man he met if he "knowed anybody that wanted to buy some hemlock back." He tried to induce Esquire Gray to go to Mr. Ainsworth and ask him about the would-be purchaser; but he was informed that Mr. Ainsworth was "up to snuff," and would keep his secret until the Deacon consented to pay the commission. He finally mounted old Charley and visited Mr. Ainsworth.

"Good mornin', Mr. Ainsworth. I guess hemlock bark won't go no higher this season, and I've concluded to let mine go, if you'll do it for a hundred and fifty dollars."

"Can't do it, Deacon."

"Say two hundred."

"No, sir. Three hundred dollars is my price."

"Three hundred 't is, then; but it's a orful price."

"Six thousand is an 'awful price' for the bark, Deacon."

"It's a purty fair price; but hemlock is hemlock, now-a-days. You can keep five thousand for the Bessie Jones morgidge, take out your three hundred, and send me the other seven by onest John, the stage driver."

"I have not seen Miss Jones since the trial; but I shall advise her to let that mortgage run. It is not due for two years, you know."

"You don't want me to pay ten per cent. intrust on that morgidge when I'll have the money to take it up? That's bearin' down too hard."

"Our motto is: 'Do as you are done by,' Deacon."

"But it ain't accordin' to Scripter."

"It is too late in the day to conduct this case 'according to Scripture.' It wasn't started on a Scriptural foundation."

"Maybe Bessie wants the money now."

"No, sir. She wrote me to retain my fee and invest the balance for her."

"How much did you tax her, Mr. Ainsworth?"

"Nothing. I thought you ought to pay her attorney's fee, and my commission for selling that bark will do it."

"You lawyers make the chips fly when you git to chargin', don't you?"

"Not always. Sometimes we simply take the bark off."

"Ain't there a law agin takin' such fees?"

"No, sir. It is lawful to charge for legal services."

"I guess I 'll go and settle with 'Squire Gray."

Deacon Wells went home to "talk it over with Elijah."

"They 've got us, father."

"Yes; and they 'll hold us, Elijah."

"Shure 's you 're born."

CHAPTER VII.

NELLIE BLUNT is crazy as a loon. She tried to kill herself last night, and they 're goin' to take her to the hospittle."

"Who told you?"

"Lige Wells."

"Well, they 'll take Lige to a wus place than that. He 'll go to State's prison, or the Provinces, before three months, for forgin' Bessie Joneses name to that deed."

"Wonder if Jim will try to clear him?"

"No. Jim will be to Congress when the trial holds, and he won't come back to git Lige out of a scrape."

"How do you know he won't?"

"'T ain't nateral for him. He ain't that kind of a feller."

"If Lige and the old Deacon depend on 'Squire Gray to clear 'em, they 'll have a fust rate chance to learn a trade."

"So they will, Sam; but they 're too smart for that. They 'll have a good lawyer."

"All the lawyers in Maine can't clear 'em. The testimony is too strong agin 'em."

" Who are the witnesses?"

" Everybody knows they done it."

" But everybody can't swear to it. Hearsay evidence won't do in a court of justice."

" Bessie Jones will swear she did n't sign the deed."

"Yes; and Jack Blunt will swear that Lige or the old Deacon did."

" They are not indicted yet."

" But they will be when the Gran' Jury meets. Jack Blunt will go before 'em. He 's desprit sense Nelly got crazy."

" What made her crazy?"

" You know that young feller that went out o' here one night last winter, as if he was sick?"

" Yes. You thought the tobacco smoke made him sick, and Zach Brown said it was something worse than that."

"That's the chap. Well, he was ingaged to Nell, and what he heered that evenin' opened his eyes, and he finally broke it off, and they played quits. Nell stood it like a major for a wile, but it finally upsot her, and she's got to go to the crazy hospittle."

"That is some of the fruits of your gossip, boys."

"'T wan't us, Uncle Henry."

"Here is Zach. Ask him who was here that evening."

"Zach, who was here the evenin' that young preacher student got sick last winter?"

Zach looked thoughtful for a moment, and replied:

"All of us, and three or four others. Lige Wells was here before the young fellow went out. Why do you ask?"

"Uncle Henry says it was our gossip that made Nell Blunt crazy."

"Uncle Henry is right. But for your slanders, Nellie Blunt would have been married before this time."

"You said as much agin her as any of us, Zach."

"That is not true, Ned. I said that she was an honest girl."

"So you did, Zach. I remember what a lecture you gave them."

"And you talked to them yourself, Uncle Henry."

"So I did, Zach. If they had heeded our advice, Nellie Blunt might have been a happy wife to-night."

"You did n't say nothin' to us 'till after the young feller went out."

"We 've cautioned you about slandering your neighbors more times than you have fingers and toes, both before and after that night. You got so bad last winter that Philip Craig would n't come in here; and he says you have almost ruined his Joe by your gossip and vulgarity."

"You talk as if you did n't want us here, Uncle Henry."

"You know you are always welcome, Sam; but I do want you to stop your gossip."

"We must talk about somethin'. You do n't want us to git as sleepy as Phil Craig, do you?"

"Philip is not asleep when his eyes are shut. He thinks more in a minute than the whole capoodle of you do in a month, except Zach Brown and Ben Love."

"You allers liked Zach and Ben better 'n the rest of us."

"That is because they don't gossip, Sam."

"Most everybody gossips, Uncle Henry."

"No they don't. Most men dislike it."

"How is it about the wimmin?"

"Women are no worse than men. A sewing circle can't hold a candle to you boys."

"You orter have been to our house yesterday. It was society day, and you'd a heered some gossip, I guess."

"Not more than I have heard here this evening."

"Yes you would. They talked about everything. We ain't a patchin' to 'em."

"They didn't slander poor Nellie Blunt."

"Yes they did. They talked wus 'en we do about her; and they said she wan't a mite crazy, but was jest makin' b'leve."

"Well; gossip's all of a piece, and 't ain't any worse in the society than in the shop."

"You can heer more to the society. I heered all about Jim Wells writin' such long letters to

Bessie Jones, and the postmaster give her one yesterday mornin’ that was longer ’n the moral law.’’

“ How do you know it was so long? ” .

“ The postmaster’s wife hefted it.”

“ He has a right to write long letters to Bessie, if he chooses.’’

“ Yes; but they say Bessie won’t appear agin the old Deacon when the Gran’ Jury meets, ’cause she ’s sot her cap for Jim.”

“ Bessie Jones is n’t the kind of girl to ‘ set her cap ’ for anybody. She is modest and lady-like.”

“ So she is, Ben; and I think the Elton gossips ought to let her alone.”

“ They say she paints —”

“ That ’s a lie. This is the second winter she has boarded at our house, and I know she do n’t paint.”

“ Landscapes. Do n’t go off half-cocked, Ben. Wait ’till I finish the sentence.”

“ Pardon me, Zach. I ought to have known better than to speak so hastily to you, for you never gossip; but I am out of patience with Sam and Dick, especially. On two or three occasions they have insinuated that Bessie Jones paints her face, and I won't hear any more of it."

"What makes her face so red some mornin's when she comes to skule?"

"She practices with her dumb-bells, about fifteen minutes, every morning before starting."

"What are dum bells, Ben?"

"Don't you know?"

"If I knowed I would n't ask."

"Shall I tell him, Ben?"

"Certainly, Zach."

"Dumb belles are pretty girls that can't talk. They never go to the society."

"Come, come, Zach. Don't join in the hue and cry against the sewing circle. Let's attend to the male gossips first."

"All right, Uncle Henry. I was simply stating a plain fact for Sam's edification."

"My edikashun's as good as your'n, Zach Brown."

"That's so, Sam; but Dick says you could n't tell what a hundred and eighty-seven pounds of haddock came to, at two and a half cents a pound."

"That's 'cause we do n't eat no haddock to our house. If it had a been codfish I could told easy enough."

"Sam, can you tell what four eggs, a pint of milk and half a loaf of bread will come to, put in a brick oven?"

"I could if I had my slate."

"I can tell without my slate."

"Well, what will they come to?"

"Custard puddin'."

"You 're jest a leetle too cute for anything, Mountain Jack. You 'd better run home and let your mamma git you to bed."

"I know when to go to bed, Sam; and that 's more 'n some of Bessie Joneses scholars knows."

"You should say 'pupils,' Jack. There are not many scholars in Elton."

"But there 's some dredful sharp men and boys, Ben. There 's Deacon Wells, for one."

"The Deacon is n't very sharp, Sam, or he would not have signed Bessie Jones' name to that deed."

"He 's sharp enough to git Bob Wallace's hog."

"How did he get Bob's hog?"

"Bob was owin' the old Deacon and could n't pay him, for the measels and hoop cough that had been in his family, so the old feller sued him. He was down to Bob's, last week, and 'spied a five-hundred-pound hog. He sot his heart on that hog, and praised Bob up wonderful, and told him he done so well raisin' hogs that he 'd give him a pig, if he 'd come for it. Bob jumped at the chance to git a pig, and offered to pay the Deacon when the children got well; but the Deacon was dredful good, and said he did n't want no pay. Bob went and got the pig, not knowin' that the law only allowed him one, and the next day the Deacon levied on the big hog, and has got him in his pen. That 's what I call purty sharp."

"That is pretty sharp for a blue-nose."

"Yes; 't will do for a genuine Yankee."

"Bob is elected for one of the Gran' Jurors, and he 'll git even with the old skin-flint when that forgin' case comes up."

"Bob is very poor, and that is a mean trick, if it is sharp."

"They say the Deacon's wife cried about it, and tried to get him to give the hog back, but he called her a blubberin' fool, and sent her out o' the room."

" He orter be ashamed of hisself."

" Folks say she 'll leave him when Jim gits marrid, and gits his new house done."

" Where did Jim git money to build that big house? He 'tends to lots of cases for nothin'."

" Look at the fee he got in that big railroad case up to Augusta! Five thousand dollars at one clip! They say he 's a lightnin' railroad lawyer."

" He 'll put it all in that house afore he gits it done. Jest look at the verandys and chickin' fixins he 's puttin' up."

" He gets a good many large fees. Jim Wells made a great deal of money last year."

" How did he git his name up so? "

" Brains, my boy. Brains will tell."

" Where did Jim git so many brains? "

" From his mother."

" Pity she could n't a served Lige in the same way."

" Lige's brains were furnished by contract, and a good deal of sawdust mixed in."

"It takes our singin' master to keep his contract."

"How so?"

"He agreed to keep skule twenty nights for twenty dollars. We chucked up nineteen dollars, and sixty cents, and he stopped the skule last night afore half past eight o'clock 'cause he said the money was expired."

"What did you learn at singing school, Sam?"

"I can rise and fall the scale, and beat time."

"It must be slow time if you can beat it, Sam."

"Time ain't so fast as you be, Mountain Jack. If it were, a streak of lightnin' could n't beat it."

"But it's too fast for a snail, Sam."

"If you was n't such a little mite of a chit, I'd take you acrost my knee, Jack."

"No danger. Catchin' before spankin' is the rule."

"I wish you's my boy for about five minutes."

"I'm glad I ain't your boy. I'd have less brains than Lige Wells has got."

"Come, boys. No quarreling."

"I don't like to be badgered by a little titmouse like him, Uncle Henry."

"You must not impose on Sam, Mountain Jack."

"I won't hurt him, Uncle Henry."

"Remember, Jack, that the doctrine that 'might makes right' is not popular in this enlightened age. You must not abuse Sam, simply because you are strong and he is weak."

"Dame Nature teaches that doctrine, Zach, however much it is at variance with our ideas."

"Where does Nature teach that 'might makes right,' Ben?"

"The birds of the air, the beasts of the field, and the fishes that inhabit the great deep, nearly all obtain their food on this principle."

"Does that make the principle right?"

"Yes; so far as it relates to the animal kingdom."

"May not animals do wrong?"

"Not when they obey a natural instinct."

"Tell us the difference, Ben, between instinct and reason."

"Instinct is a faculty, or aptitude, with which

animals are indued, while reason is confined to man."

"Yes, I see. Certain animals build habitations and provide stores for the winter. They know, instinctively, that winter is coming, and they wisely make provision for it. Man does the same thing, and we call it reason. The difference between instinct and reason is as clear as mud."

"Yet there is a difference, Zach, 'though I'll admit the line is not clearly defined."

"The animals has the best of it these times. A poor man can't lay in enough to take him through the winter, onless he's pertickerler ekernomical."

"Poor men can't afford to practice economy, Sam."

"Can't afford it?"

"No, sir."

"Git out with your nonsense, Ben. They're the very fellers that has to afford it."

"A poor man buys cheap goods for his family. It costs as much to make up a cheap as a good piece, and it will not wear half as long. Take, for instance, a piece of sheeting. The poor man buys a poor piece for ten cents per yard, because he can't afford to buy a good piece at fourteen cents. His wife can't make it up and do the work in a family of six or seven children, so he hires it done. There is but little wear in the goods, and in a few weeks it is gone, while the fourteen-cent sheeting would wear for months. So you see, Sam, a poor man can't afford to be economical."

"There is somethin' in it; but poor men's children is orful extravagant. There's Hez Godfry's boy allers comes to skule with baked beans loose in his pocket, right among his slate pencils."

"I should think they'd wet his pocket."

"No. He takes the dry ones from the top of the pot."

"I'm glad to learn that one of your school mates ' knows beans,' Sam."

"That's all he knows. His father was down on buildin' the skule house, and that's why I'm down on his father. He made a speech at the skule meetin', and said too much learnin' made boys sassy. He said I were sassy; and if a man cut a cord of kiln wood and put it on the warf, that was a dollar; and if he went a trip to Bosting with Cap'n Smith, that was twelve dollars more, and twelve dollars and one dollar made thirteen dollars; and that was enough edikashun for any fool. But when the vote was took the old feller was all by hisself, and that made him rothy, so he did n't send his boy for some time, and when he did send him, Gus Bruce, the master, give him an orful floggin', and he took him out." ·

"I did n't blame him for that. Gus flogged the wrong boy."

"Yes; but he went and polygized like a little man, and took it all back, and it did n't satisfy the old feller. He said Gus orter took back the lickin'; and he'll let that boy grow up in ignorance afore he'll send to a teacher that he do n't like. I'm agin anybody that's agin skulin' their children. That's me, right out, and mam's proud o' my pinyuns on the subject."

"I am glad your mother has the courage to feel proud of you, Sam."

"So 'm I, Zach. A boy feels lots better when folks is proud of him."

"Your mother ain't folks. She's only one people, Sam."

"Now see here, Jack. I do n't want no more o' your sass here to-night."

"Take it home to eat on your pan-cakes, Sam."

"I have somethin' better 'n pan-cakes to eat to home."

"Pan-cakes is cheap fillin', Sam, and your father orter keep you on 'em."

"Mam says they ain't good brain food, and she do n't make 'em."

"What do you think of this idea about fish for brain food, Ben?"

"It's a humbug, Zach. Our fishermen, who have little else to eat, have n't brains enough to tell when their feet are cold."

"Mam says codfish is good brain food."

"What does your father say about it, Sam?"

"His father thinks brains orter be fed on pertaters, so 'twixt 'em both they keep Sam on codfish hash."

"There's wus eatin' than codfish hash, Jack, and some famlys in Elton knows it."

"They say they just live on it up to Deacon Wellses."

"Who says so, Tom?"

" Bob Crane told me. The old Deacon hired him to cut wood for forty cents a cord and boarded. He could stan' the forty cents for cuttin' wood, but he got tired livin' on codfish hash."

"I should think the Deacon's wife would want something better."

" So she does; but Bob says every time she cooked anything else the Deacon would make a fuss about it, and tell her hash was good enough for these hard times."

" That explodes your fish for brain food theory, Zach. Lige Wells has been raised on a fish diet, and he will not die of brain fever."

"Jim was raised the same way, and he has more brains than a dozen ordinary men."

" But he was born with brains. I do n't claim that fish will destroy a man's brains."

"If it did, Sam Smith's would be gone long ago."

" And you 'd have nothin' for the fish to begin on, Jack."

" Come, boys; do n't be personal. A little more brains would n't hurt either of you."

" It takes an eight-inch hat for me, Uncle
Henry."

" Your brains is like the rum Deacon Wells
give Jack Blunt, Sam.   They 're thinned out
with water."

" Hold on, Jack.   You mus n't be impudent."

" I ain't any wus than Sam, Uncle Henry."

" But you must set Sam a good example,
Jack."

" If I do, he won't foller it.   He 's allers fol-
lerin' his big nose."

" Mam says all the great men has big noses.
Our minister 's got a picter of Washington
Irvin' and his friends, and they all has big
noses, like mine."

" So does the great men in Elton.   There 's
Deacon Wells, Tom Siddons, Lige Wells and
Sam Smith."

" Your own nose ain't so orful small, Dick."

" That 's so, Sam; but it ain't big enough to
take me in with you great men."

" There 's another dig at the Lord's handwriting, Uncle Henry."

" You must consider what He has to write on,
Ben.   I do n't claim that you can always read

a man's heart by looking at his face, but it is generally a very good index."

"Sometimes children inherit the features of one parent and the brains of the other."

"Not often.   Look at the Wells family.   Lige has the features and even less brains than his father, while Jim has the features and brains of his mother."

"I am not acquainted with Mrs. Wells, but if she has so much brain I should think she might influence her husband."

"An angel could n't control the old Deacon. She submits because she thinks it would disgrace her children if she should leave him."

"She can't disgrace Lige."

"No; but she thinks the world of Jim."

"Jim wants her to leave the old Deacon, and offered to provide for her, I 'm told."

"Yes.   He wanted her to go when he left home; but she thinks it 's her duty to stay.   The Deacon is getting worse and worse every year, and she will either go to Heaven or get a divorce before long.   No woman can stand what she does, and live many years."

"They say Lige is worse than the old man."

"I guess the difference between them is like the difference between Satan and the devil. They 're both as bad as they can be."

"If I 's her, I 'd pizen their coffee and send 'em home."

"There 's no place for them to go to, Dick. That question was settled last winter."

"She can't pizen their coffee, 'cause they do n't drink none."

" What do they drink?"

" Warm water, sweeten'd with merlasses, is their reg'lar drink, but they have buttermilk when there 's no sale for it."

" They say the Deacon sends all the butter to Glenville and sells it, and do n't leave his wife any to put on the table."

" And Lige hides all the eggs."

" I guess 't ain't quite so bad as that, boys."

" Bob Crane says 't is, and he orter know."

" The Deacon and Lige is wus than ever sense Jim left home. They do n't give Mis Wells a minit's peace."

" How do they do when quarterly conference comes, and the Deacon has company?"

" They do n't go to see the Deacon no more.

He's so crusty every time his wife kills a pullet
that they do n't want to go and see him. They
git better grub som'ers else."

" Ain't they goin' to haul the Deacon over the
coals for forgin' that deed?"

" He told 'em, last conference, that he was
ready for trial. They summoned Bessie Jones,
and she would n't appear agin him. She said
she did n't want to mix up in church matters;
but mam thinks she's goin' to git marrid to
Jim, and that's why she's so shy about it."

" I do n't blame her for trying to keep out of
a quarrel; but seems to me she ought to go and
tell what she knows about the old rascal."

" She says she do n't know who signed her
name to that deed, Uncle Henry. She has
her opinion about it, but her opinion is n't
evidence."

" That's so, Ben; but I guess she knows who
did it."

" Why do n't they summon Jack Blunt?
He 'll tell."

" They was goin' to; but the Deacon told 'em
they could n't try one of the Lord's anninted
with unbelievin' witnesses, and the minister

agreed with him, on the ground that it wan't Scripteral."

" Mam says she do n't see what the minister sticks and hangs for the old Deacon so hard for. It 's preshus little salary he pays."

" Maybe he thinks if he sticks up to him he 'll pay more."

The entrance of Philip, the philosopher, was the signal for the gossips to cease. He caught the drift of the conversation, however, and remarked:

" That is uncharitable, Tom. It is very natural for a pastor to consider his flock inno-cent, and if he really believes the Deacon is innocent he ought to stick up to him, regard-less of the amount of money he pays."

" But he can't believe him innocent, Philip, if he has taken any trouble to investigate his case. Everybody in the village, who heard what the evidence was before the court, thinks the old rascal is guilty; even his own church members."

" Possibly the minister has not investigated, Uncle Henry. Why not take the charitable view of it, and give him the benefit of the doubt?"

"That's right, Phil. I've no doubt the minister knows he's guilty, and I'm willin' to give him the benefit of it."

"I spoke to Uncle Henry, Tom."

"I know you did; but I answered you, Phil. Ain't that jest as well?"

"No. I wanted his opinion, not yours."

"Well, Philip, it's my opinion that Deacon Wells is guilty, and the minister knows it. I don't believe Parson Green would attempt to shield a guilty member of his church."

"I know he wouldn't; and I don't believe Elder Steele would, either. Elder Steele is a good man, and I honor him for sticking to the Deacon so long as he believes him innocent. I wouldn't give a snap for a friend that would desert me simply because the gossips of Elton pronounced me guilty; and you're the only man, except the gossips, that I have heard express an opinion about Deacon Wells' guilt or innocence. Uncle Henry."

"Father says he's guilty, Phil, and he's a member of his church in good standin'. He says he'd believe anything Jack Blunt would say about the old Deacon."

"I presume there are many better men than Jack Blunt or Deacon Wells; but I am not prepared to condemn Elder Steele for believing the Deacon innocent. If Deacon Wells is guilty, Elder Steele is deceived."

"You have more charity for him than I, Philip. I do n't see how he can help believing him guilty."

"How can I help believing him guilty? Uncle Henry?"

"Do you believe him innocent?"

"I do n't know what to believe. The law presumes that every man is innocent until his guilt is proved. I want to be as charitable as the law; yet I do not consider Deacon Wells an honest man; but you must remember that Elder Steele, during his short stay in Elton, has heard comparatively little about him, and is doubtless deceived in regard to his true character. What I object to, is this wholesale denunciation of Elder Steele."

"I never see you at his church, Phil."

"That is n't the place to get acquainted with a minister. I have spent several evenings in his company, and have learned more about him in a single evening than I would by attending his church for a year."

" I should think 't would be kinder dry goin' to see a minister."

"That depends on who goes, Dick. My most enjoyable evenings are spent with Parson Green and Elder Steele. They are first rate fellows, and I always feel at home in their company."

" Ain't they allers teasin' you about religion?"

" We sometimes talk upon religious subjects; but they seldom introduce anything of the kind. They are too sensible to bore their visitors with long sermons."

" Don't the Bible teach that a minister should labor in season and out of season, Philip?"

" Perhaps it does, Uncle Henry; but it says nothing about what he shall do between times, when his friends call in to spend the evening."

" There ought to be no ' between times ' in a minister's life, Philip."

" There 's where you 're wrong, Uncle Henry. Parson Green has accomplished as much ' between times ' as in the pulpit. His social qualities have drawn many young Eltonians into the fold. They could not be reached in any other way, and the Parson knew it. He did not drive them from him by constantly talking about the sin that is in the world; but entered into their sports with the enthusiasm of a school boy. More than half of the young people in the village are members of his church."

"Yes; but that is the result of his work in the pulpit."

"Nonsense, Uncle Henry. He might have preached 'till doomsday without converting them if they had not loved him. He has saved as many souls by playing base ball as in any other way."

"Maybe he has, Philip. I wish he could get a few more."

"They do n't play base ball."

"Some of us does. Ben Love and Zach Brown is allers playin'. Why do n't Parson Green git them?"

"'Cause Ben 's a Methodist and Zach 's a blacksmith. They 're too heavy for one man to fetch."

"Better be a blacksmith than a loafer, Sam."

"There ain't but little odds, and the loafer gits what little there is."

"You ought to learn a trade, Sam."

"What do I want of a trade, Phil? Mam says I 'm goin' to collige bimeby."

"Your mother is right, Sam. If there is n't enough in a boy to make a mechanic he ought to go through college."

"I guess there 's the makin' of a mechanic in me, Zach, if I wanted a trade. I 'd ruther be a lawyer or somethin'."

"You 've got a sure thing on the ' or something,' Sam, and you 'd better hang to it."

"That 's what mam says."

"Every boy should learn a trade, either before or after he goes through college."

"Why, Phil?"

"Because, no boy is educated until he knows how to earn his bread."

"Is it wise for a boy, who is trying to qualify himself for a profession, to spend three or four years in learning a trade?"

"I think it is, Ben. Three-fourths of our college graduates are never heard from after they receive their diploma, simply because they have not learned to work."

"What becomes of them?"

"They choose a profession, enter the lists with mechanics who have educated themselves by lamp-light, and fail. After a disgraceful failure they manage to get a clerkship, or some unimportant position, and never rise above it. It is better to be a good mechanic than to hang on to the tail end of a profession."

"That's true; but I don't see how learning a trade helps to qualify a man for a profession."

"It's good discipline, Ben. They have learned to work, and that's half the battle. Our most successful professional men are mechanics, who entered their profession with a determination to succeed, backed up by a good constitution and physical strength, attributable to the work-bench. A certain kind of independence is essential if a man would succeed; and no man is independent until he has learned a trade."

"I don't want no trade. Mam says I'll be a ornamental member of a profeshun."

"Your mother is right, Sam. You'll never make a useful member."

"I guess I'll be as good a lawyer or somethin' as you are blacksmith."

12

"You 'd make a fust rate butcher, Sam."

"Why, Jack?"

"'Cause you 'd never have to run after a calf. They 'd come right to you."

"Come, boys. You 're getting too personal again. You must behave yourselves."

"I can't learn Sam to behave hisself, Uncle Henry."

"You commenced on Sam this time, Mountain. I was listening."

"Was I sassy, Uncle Henry?"

"That 's what they used to call it when I was a boy."

"But 't ain't fair to go so fur back."

"It would be a good thing for all you boys if you had to go back a generation or two. We had to toe the mark when I was a little codger. 'Children should be seen, not heard,' was the motto in the good old days; but everything has changed for the worse, 'specially boys."

Uncle Henry notified the boys that he was going to close up. He put out the light, locked the rickety door, and went home, fully impressed with the idea that "everything had changed for the worse, 'specially boys."

CHAPTER VIII.

RETRIBUTION.

G O before the Grand Jury and make a clean breast of it, Jack. You shall not be prosecuted."

"On them terms I'll do it, Mr. King. The old Deacon hain't treated me right, and Lige had as much to do with Nelly goin' crazy as anybody. I do n't care a continental cuss if they both git into the penitenshary. They'll know how to treat a feller when they come out."

"The Grand Jury will meet next Monday. Shall I send a subpœna for you, or will you appear voluntarily?"

"Oh, I'll make a volunteer job of it, and swear from July to dog days, if you want me to."

"What is the ground for your grievance, Jack?"

"I've got ground for half a dozen grievances

and enough for a big pertater patch besides. He's lied to me more 'n a thousand times. He promised me the mill on the Jones place if I'd apprize it for one-third of what it were wuth, and then when I done his dirty work he backed down."

" So you appraised the place for one-third its real value, did you, Jack? "

" Yes; me and Tom Siddons done it. The old Deacon only give us fifty dollars for the job. That's another grievance I've got agin him."

" Did he make a bargain with you beforehand, and tell you what he wanted you to do? "

" Yes; me and Tom Siddons."

" Where does Tom Siddons live? "

" Up to Sackarap."

" Will he swear that the Deacon paid him money to make a false appraisement? "

" He 'll swear like the d—l agin the Deacon. The old cuss cheated him out of his best cow."

" How did he do it? "

" He swapped Tom three Sandy Ridge shoats for Pole and China. Tom do n't know no more about live hogs than the Deacon does about the Scripter, and when he found out the old feller'd cheated him he was orful rothy, and he ain't got over it yit."

" Then the Deacon is a hard customer?"

" Yes, sir; he's a hard ticket. He'd do well enough up to Sackarap, where they're all hard, but he's a orful poor stick to make a deacon out of. He's consider'bly sap rotted."

" I should think Elder Steele would haul him over the coals."

" Coals wo n't have no effect on him. He can stan' brimstone and niter gliserin'. He's tough-er 'n a blue-nosed mule."

" What's a blue-nosed mule, Jack?"

" Do n't you know?"

" No, sir; I do not."

" Well that's sing'lar, shure enough. You're a lawyer and do n't know what a blue-nosed mule is. It's a mule raised among the blue-noses in the Provinces, Mr. King."

" Sure enough. I ought to have known that."

" I s'pose lawyers can 't learn it all, but they generally know most everything."

" Has the Deacon any other bad habits beside forging deeds and cheating his neighbors in hog trades?"

"Yes. He plays cards and smuggles rum."

"Is he good at cards?"

"No, sir; he's bad at 'em. He do n't play no fair game, but Lige has got so he can beat him playin' ten cent ante."

"Does Deacon Wells play cards with his own son?"

"Not any more. Lige beat him out of half a dollar three or four times, hand runnin', and the old feller wo n't play agin him sense."

"Who does he play with?"

"Them Bangor chaps."

"Does Elder Steele know that he plays cards?"

"I guess not. Nobody but Lige and me knowed it for a long time. When he went back on me about the mill I told some of the boys, but I guess they kep it to theirselves."

"Does he smuggle much rum?"

"Not so much late years as he used to."

"Where does he land it?"

"To Bangor."

"How did you find out that he smuggled rum, Jack?"

"He got sick one fall, and I went down and got it for him."

" Did the revenue officers disturb him? "

" One of 'em watched him purty clost, but the Deacon give him a hoss and carridge, and he could n't see nothin' after'ards."

" Do you know his name? "

" Yes; but I wo n't tell, and he 's out now, anyhow, so it would n't do you no good."

" All right, Jack. I 'm very much obliged for what you have told. I never dreamed that Deacon Wells was such a man as you represent him. I supposed this forgery was his first offense, and was disposed to deal leniently with him; but I shall prosecute him to the bitter end, now."

" Look out for your jury, Mr. King, or he 'll buy 'em all up right afore your face and eyes."

" I 'll keep a sharp look out, Jack. Be on hand next Monday."

" I will."

Jack Blunt appeared before the Grand Jury at the appointed time, and told all he knew about the forgery. Bessie Jones was an unwilling witness, and stated that she did not sign the deed. This was all she knew about it. Somebody was guilty of forgery, but she could not determine in her own mind who was the guilty party. If it was Deacon Wells, she thought he had been sufficiently punished by making restitution, and if consistent with the ends of justice she preferred that the matter might be dropped. So far as she was concerned she did not desire to prosecute him.

The Jury looked at the matter in a different light, and found a true bill against Hezekiah and Elijah Wells on the testimony of Jack Blunt. Jack's evidence was conclusive. He told his story in a straightforward manner, detailing the conversation that was held both before and after signing the deed. He did not try to shield himself, but "made a clean breast of it." He was cross-examined by one of the jurors, but the attempt to shake his evidence simply made it stronger, and when the vote was taken it was unanimous.

A warrant was issued for the arrest of the guilty parties, and placed in the hands of the sheriff, who lost no time in serving it. Assisted by his deputy he made the arrest when the Deacon and Elijah were at the dinner table. They submitted quietly; but when the officers produced the handcuffs, Patience Wells begged

" *She plead that they might be spared this indignity.*"
— Page 185.

them, with tears in her eyes, to desist, assuring them that the prisoners would go with them without resistance. She forgot their cruelty, and only remembered that she was a wife and mother, as she plead that they might be spared this indignity.

" Don't be a fool, Patience. We'll be back to-morrer. We're as innersent as a lamb, ain't we, Elijah?"

" Yes, mother; we're innersent as a hull flock of sheep, and they'll find, when they git us to Glenville, that they've ketched the wrong pigs by the ears."

The kind hearted sheriff pitied the sorrowing wife, and put the handcuffs in his pocket. He hurried his prisoners off, and handcuffed them as soon as they were out of the village. By request of Deacon Wells the sheriff sent word to Esquire Gray to come immediately to Glenville. It was five o'clock when the party drove up to the jail. Deacon Wells was surprised to find that the jailor was a former citizen of Elton.

" Well, Deacon, I'm sorry to number you among my boarders; but I suppose you'll be bailed out to-morrow."

"I do n't want to be bailed out. I'd ruther be filled up. I did n't half finish my dinner."

"I 'll see that you are filled up, Elijah, in short order. I 'll have your supper here inside of ten minutes."

"I s'pose you 'll let us out to eat, Jesse?"

"Can 't do it, Deacon. I 'm sorry; but it 's against the rules to take a prisoner out to meals."

"But we ain't prisoners, Jesse."

"You are for the time being, and I shall have to treat you as I do the others. I can 't show any partiality, you know. They 'd cut my head off if I did."

"But Elijah and me is innersent, Jesse."

"I hope so, Deacon, and if you are, you will have no trouble in proving it; so you won't have long to stay, even if you ain't bailed out."

"We do n't have to prove our innersence, Jesse. They 've got to prove we 're guilty, and they can 't do it. Who 's the witnesses agin us?"

"I believe Jack Blunt is the principal witness."

"His witnessin' won't amount to nothin', father. Everybody knows he 's a orful liar."

"I want you to write to him, Jesse. Tell him to come up right off. Put this five dollar note in to pay his bill, and tell him I 'm orful anxious to see him."

"Perhaps you 'd better wait a day or two, Deacon. You may be bailed out, and then you can see him."

"Jesse 's right, father. Jack 's a feller that 's better seen than writ to."

"So he is, Elijah. I 'll see him when I git out."

"You do n't 'spect us to sleep in here all night, do you, Jes.?"

"I 'm afraid you 'll have to, Elijah."

"I do n't care nothin' for myself, but it 's hard on dad."

"I can stan' as much as you can, Elijah."

"Can you give a feller a chaw of terbacker, Jes.? I left mine to home."

"Here 's some genuine James river, Elijah. You can keep the plug."

"Does the county buy your terbacker, Jes.?"

"No. Why do you ask?"

"'Cause I thought you 's orful free with it."

"Tobacco is like a joke in shearin' time, you know, Elijah; free to all."

"I 'm glad that 's one of your rules, Jes., for I chaw a orful sight."

"Do you chew, Deacon?"

"Jest a little, Jesse; but you need n't mind me.   I can borry from Elijah."

"All right.   I 'll go and bring in your supper."

"Bring enough of it, Jes.; and I guess you 'd better bring a pack of cards.   Maybe dad 'll be lonesome."

"You know I do n't b'leve in playin' cards, Elijah."

"I know; but maybe you 'll git tired doin' nothin' and will play jest to make the time seem shorter."

"I 'll bring them, Deacon, and you can do as you choose about playing."

"Jest as you 're mind to, Jesse."

The cards were brought, but the Deacon would not play. He did not feel like indulging in a game of draw poker on his first evening in jail. He did not fear the result of the trial; but he trembled as he thought of what the public would say. He passed a sleepless night, and waited anxiously for Esquire Gray to call next day. Elijah slept as soundly as any of the hardened criminals by whom he was surrounded. He did not realize his danger, and he passed the morning in playing cards with one of his fellow prisoners. About noon Esquire Gray was ushered in by the accommodating jailor.

"Hello, Deacon; they've got you in limbo, have they?"

"Got me in jail, you'd better say, 'Squire; and I want to git out."

"All right. I'll bail you out, but you must deed me enough of your property to secure me."

"Secure you agin what?"

"Against your failure to appear for trial."

"I'll be shure to appear."

"I presume you will; but we lawyers always take property as a mere matter of form, and deed it back when the trial is over."

"What property do you want me to deed you?"

"Your home place, the Bently farm, the township of timber land and the old Smith farm."

"Had n't you better take all I 've got?"

"I shall deed it all back if you stand your trial, so what difference does it make about the amount?"

"All right, 'Squire. Draw up your deed as soon as you can. I want to git out."

The deed was executed and the Deacon and Elijah liberated. The crafty lawyer placed the deed in the pocket of his great coat, with a twinkle in his snake-like eye that augured mischief. It was a "mere matter of form" that was destined to cause serious inconvenience to Deacon Wells.

"Well, Patience, we 're back agin jest as I told you, and you look as if you 'd been cryin' for a fortni't."

"Is it all over? Are you clear of the charge?"

"We hain't had our trial; but it will be a mere matter of form, as 'Squire Gray says. We 'll be cleared easy enough when the trial comes off."

"I hope so."

"I *know* so, Patience, and that orter satisfy any reasonable woman; but there 's no satisfyin' wimmin; is there, Elijah?"

"No, father; wimmin is wimmin, and you can't make men of 'em, no how."

"Hurry up and git supper, Patience. I must go and see Jack Blunt. He's the witness agin us."

"What are you charged with, Deacon?"

"We ain't charged with anything, Patience."

"What were you arrested for? I was so excited, yesterday, that I did n't ask."

"For forgin' a deed; and we never done it. Bessie Jones signed that deed her own self, and Jack Blunt will swear to it."

"Will Bessie Jones swear that she did n't sign it?"

"I s'pose so; but no jury orter take a woman's swear agin a man's; and Jack Blunt's a Justice of the Peace."

Patience Wells knew that an intelligent jury would believe Bessie Jones, and she felt that James' prophecy would be fulfilled. How distinctly she remembered his words: "Your avarice will lead you to a fellon's cell, and your ill-gotten wealth will not unlock its door." Her life had indeed been full of sorrow, but the most poignant grief awaited her. How gladly she would rest; yet the Angel of Death cruelly passed her by.

"Good evenin', Jack.   Is nobody 'round?"

"You know there's nobody here but me. You know Nelly is in the crazy hospittle."

"That 's all the better, for I want a little talk with you.   What made you swear agin Elijah and me afore the Gran' Jury?"

"'Cause I had to."

"Now I 've a propersishun to make."

"Les hear it."

"I will give you fifty dollars to swear afore the court that Bessie Jones signed that deed."

"I can't do it, Deacon.   I 've quit lyin'."

"Then I 'll give you a hundred to go down to the Provinces and keep hid 'till after the trial."

"Can't do it, Deacon.   Mr. King would send for me.   He knows the ropes."

"Then you 're goin' to swear agin' us at court?"

"I s'pose so."

"If you do I 'll send you to the penitenshary for smugglin' rum, forgin' that acknoligment, and false apprisin' the Jones place."

"Scoot ahead, Deacon.   I ain't a carin' what

becomes of me. What have I got to live for?
I'd willingly go to prison for the sake of seein'
you and Lige there. He was the cause of Nelly
goin' crazy, and I'll have my revenge, anyhow."

"Hain't I allers treated you like a man,
Jack?"

"No. You promised me the mill to run, and
backed out. You kep me doin' dirty work on
preshus little pay."

"I'll give you the mill to run after the trial's
over, if you'll go away and not swear agin us."

"Once a liar, allers a liar, is my motto, Deacon. I shan't trust you no more."

"All right, Jack. You swear agin us and
I'll make you smart for it; that's all."

"I'm smart enough now to send you and
Lige up, and I'll do it."

"I'll git 'Squire Gray to have your commishun took back."

"Don't trouble yourself, Deacon. I'll quit
and come up to prison to hecter you and Lige."

Deacon Wells went home to "make Patience
smart." The cowardly villain had a way of
making his wife particularly uncomfortable
when any of his plans were frustrated.

“ What did Jack say, Deacon ? ”

“ It ’s none of your bizness what he said. It ’s strange that wimmin can’t mind their own bizness and stop meddlin’ with other people.”

And Patience resolved to “ mind her own business.”

’Squire Gray was not an attorney; he was simply a pettifogger, and when Deacon Wells asked him to see Jack Blunt he readily assented, but his influence was exerted for the prosecution, and he only confirmed Jack in his resolution to appear against the Deacon. He wanted his client convicted; not that the ends of justice might be subserved, but he had that “ mere matter of form ” safely deposited in his side pocket, where it often came in contact with an itching palm. He persuaded the Deacon that additional counsel would be an unnecessary expense without corresponding benefit. In this, however, he was right, for all the attorneys in the State could not have saved the Deacon from the penalty of his crime.

“ Put up a lunch for me and Elijah, Patience,

and be in a hurry about it. We must go to court to-day."

"Put in some biled aigs for me, mother."

"There are no eggs in the house, Elijah. You sold them all, on Saturday."

"Can't you borry a few from Mis Craig? A lunch with no biled aigs in it ain't wuth eatin', 'cordin' to my noshun."

"I will go and see her."

"Let Elijah go, Patience. You'll fool 'round talkin' with Mis Craig 'till we'll be late."

"So she will. I'll go myself, father."

"Git your water hot and bile 'em in a hurry when Elijah gits back. Come; fly 'round."

"The water is hot, and I won't detain you, Deacon. Have you employed any one to assist Mr. Gray in your defense?"

"No. He says 't would be money throwed away, and I know he's enough for any on 'em."

"I wish you would get Mr. Ainsworth to help him."

"You're a fool, Patience, and don't know nothin' about law. I wish you'd mind your own bizness and not meddle so much."

Patience regretted that she had not adhered to her resolution to "mind her own business."

Deacon Wells and Elijah entered the court room as the Judge was calling the docket. After the usual delay in impanneling the jury, the State called Bessie Jones and Jack Blunt. Their testimony was the same as given before the Grand Jury, and the witnesses for the defense were sworn. Elder Steele testified that, "so far as he knew Deacon Wells, he was an upright man and a Christian." Two or three members of the church also testified to the Deacon's good character; but when Brother Smith was called to the stand he remembered "that hoss trade," and he swore, positively, that "he had knowed Deacon Wells for nigh onto twenty year, and he did n't believe he had an honest hair in his head, except the wig he bought to Bangor."

Some of the jurors were acquainted with the Deacon, and they agreed with Brother Smith. Jack Blunt's testimony was convincing. The Judge's charge was impartial, but he gave the impression that little doubt existed, in his mind, as to the guilt of the accused. The jury retired in charge of a bailiff, and returned in twenty minutes with a verdict of "guilty."

The prisoners were remanded to the county jail, a motion for a re-hearing overruled, and on the following day they were sentenced by the Judge. The Deacon was shocked when the Judge, after a moral lecture, sentenced him to "seven years' confinement in the penitentiary." For the first time, since the commencement of the trial, he realized that "the way of the transgressor is hard." Broken in spirit, and weeping as only the guilty can weep, he left the court room, assisted by a bailiff.

The Judge wisely considered Elijah's birth and surroundings, and sentenced him to four years' imprisonment. This was a lighter penalty than he hoped for, after his father's sentence, and he looked rather pleased, than otherwise, when the judgment was pronounced. He went to the jail with a firm step, requesting the jailor to give him a good dinner, as he was "orful hungry."

"Well, father, them four aces was beat bad, wasn't they?"

"Yes; Jack Blunt beat 'em, and I 'll git even with him yit."

"I 've got a year for every ace, and I wish Jack Blunt had the pot."

"I 'll give him a wus pot than you 've got, Elijah. I 'll send him up for smugglin' rum. I 'll learn him better 'n to swear agin me."

In due time the Sheriff took the prisoners to Thomaston, to work for the Commonwealth. When the prison garb was produced, the Deacon kindly offered to "buy his own close," a proposition which was promptly rejected by the official. Elijah protested. He said his father was "innersent as a sheep, and a deacon in good standin', and them close would n't look well on him." The obliging official informed him that his father might wear the clothes as a badge of innocence, if he chose; but he must put on the regulation suit.

Six months have passed since Deacon Wells and Elijah entered upon the life for which they are so eminently fitted. James has returned from Washington, and is busy with professional cares. He has induced his mother to take charge of his new house, and they are living cosily together, 'though both feel keenly the disgrace that has come through the conduct of the Deacon and Elijah. The world is not ready for an unqualified indorsement of the wholesome adage, "A man can disgrace only himself."

James has a great deal of "business at Berwick," and he spends as many pleasant hours with Bessie Jones as his busy life will permit. She is enjoying her vacation, and is trying to master Greek. Harry tells her she has "mastered a Congressman," and her ambition should be satisfied.

CHAPTER IX.

WELL, DEACON, I got your letter, and here I am."

"You've been a good wile comin', 'Squire."

"I was detained by a perplexing lawsuit."

"Law suits is most allers perplexin,' ain't they? Leastwise, mine has been."

"They usually perplex the client more than the attorney, but mine was perplexing to both."

"What was the matter? Had n't the feller nothin' to pay fees with?"

"I was both client and attorney, Deacon. There was no fee in the case."

"I s'pose you hain't no appertite for lawin' without money, have you, 'Squire?"

"Not much, Elijah."

"Stop your foolin', Elijah, and let 'Squire and me git to bizness."

"What can I do for you, Deacon?"

"The Warden says you can see the Gov'ner and git me and Elijah pardoned out o' here."

"That 's easier said than done, Deacon."

"It 's the same Gov'ner that appinted Jack Blunt, ain't it?"

"Yes; he 's on his third term now."

"Then you can fetch him. 'Tain't no more work to pardon me and Elijah than 't is to appint a justice, 'specially such a one as Jack Blunt."

"But the Governor do n't like to take the responsibility of exercising the pardoning power, and it will cost me a great deal of money to get you pardoned."

"How much will you have to pay him?"

"I won't have to pay the Governor anything. He 's an honest man, and I would n't dare to offer him a bribe; but I 'll have to get the jury, the Judge, and the court officers to sign a petition for your pardon, and that will take a great deal of time and money. I 'll make you a proposition, Deacon."

"Les heer it."

"I 'll undertake your case, spend my own

money, and if I fail it will be my loss; if I succeed I will keep the Bently farm, the township of timber land, and the old Smith farm, and I will deed you back your home place."

"That's a orful propersishun, 'Squire. The property is wuth thirty thousand dollars. We'd better stay our time out and have somethin' when we do git out."

"That may do for you, Elijah, for you've only three years and a half to stay; but your father has six years and a half, and that, in this place, will be equivalent to his life time."

"If he's goin' to die poor, he might as well die here as anywhere."

"So I had, Elijah. I'll never give it."

"All right, Deacon. I'll bid you good day. Stay here six months longer and you'll be glad to come to my terms."

"Hold on, 'Squire. I'll give you the old Smith farm."

"No, sir."

"I'll give you the old Smith farm and the Bently farm."

"Don't do it, father. They're wuth five or

six thousand dollars, and a thousand dollars a year is big pay for stayin' here."

"I can make that much speckerlatin' if I 's out o' here."

"All right, 'Squire. Dad 'll let 'em go."

"But I can't take them, Elijah. I shall adhere to my first proposition."

"I won't give it, 'Squire."

"All right. Good day. Let me hear from you when you want to get out."

The avaricious pettifogger went home and drew up a petition for the pardon of Hezekiah and Elijah Wells. He secured the signatures of the jurors by appealing to their sympathy for Mrs. Wells. He found it more difficult to get the names of the court officers and members of the bar, but finally succeeded in procuring a majority of them by a free utterance of the magical name of James Wells. James was deservedly popular with them, and the unscrupulous apology for a lawyer took advantage of this, in order to further his interest. James knew nothing about the proceedings, and Esquire Gray used his name without authority. He had Deacon Wells in his power, and if he could not secure the valuable timber land he would take the farms; but he "calculated" that the old Deacon would accept his proposition, and he was not mistaken. His papers were barely perfected when a letter was received from Deacon Wells stating that he "would take the propersishun, but it was orful hard. Elijah didn't want him to do it, but he couldn't stay there no longer." Esquire Gray wrote an agreement, visited the prison, procured the Deacon's signature, and then went to see the Governor.

———

"Good morning, Governor."

"Good morning, Esquire Gray. How do you do?"

"Well, I thank you."

"I'm really glad to see you. Take a seat."

"Are you at leisure this morning?"

"I am to meet some friends from Portland at eleven o'clock. I shall be at leisure until that hour. Can I do anything for you?"

"Yes, sir. I have a petition here for the pardon of Deacon Wells and his son, Elijah."

" Deacon Wells is the father of Congressman Wells, is he not? "

" Yes, sir."

" The penitentiary is an odd place for a deacon."

" Yes, sir; but he is an odd kind of a deacon, although his punishment was altogether too severe."

" I have almost forgotten the circumstances. I believe he was convicted on a charge of forgery? "

" Yes, sir; for forging a deed. He had purchased the property at Sheriff's sale, but no notice had been served on one of the heirs, and the Deacon signed her name to the deed. He is a very ignorant man, and did not realize the magnitude of the crime."

" How does it come that his son is so bright? He has made a good record in Congress."

" He takes after his mother."

" How is the other son? "

" He knows even less than his father. He was considered the greatest dunce in the village."

"Did James Wells speak of visiting me in the interest of his father?"

"No, sir. He thought I had better come. He feels a little hesitancy about asking a favor of you. You know he supported your opponent for the nomination. He spoke of you in flattering terms; but John Vale was an old college mate of Jim's, and he had to support him. We took a sharp tilt at each other on your account, and it created a little feeling between us; but it's all over now. Jim has a great deal of influence in our part of the State, and by granting this pardon you will make him your fast friend."

"I thought there was a little feeling between you after the Congressional Convention had adjourned?"

"Oh, no. There's no truth in the report that I did n't support him. I voted for him."

"I never heard that you did n't vote for him. I was told that a little feeling existed after the nomination."

"I suppose every man feels a little sore after a defeat; but Jim and 1 are all right now."

"That's right, Esquire. There's nothing like pulling together in the harness."

"You'll find us ready to pull together when you want our services, Governor."

"Thank you. I always look for a good report from your town, Esquire."

"In future, as in the past, you will find me ready to work for my friends, Governor."

"How does everything look down there this year?"

"Very flattering, indeed. We are all wide awake, and will roll up a larger majority for you than ever."

"I am glad to hear it, for I shall need all the votes I can get. The opposition are giving me a hard fight this year."

"I know it's an 'off year,' but you need not fear the result."

"They are trying to force me to take a position on the question of Free Trade."

"Why don't you do it? Free Trade is popular with us, and you would gain largely by declaring in favor of it."

"But there are conflicting interests. The ship builders in your locality, as elsewhere, favor

Free Trade, while our manufacturers demand protection."

"I did n't think of that. Can't you perform the great political two-horse act?"

"That will do in National, but not in State politics."

"Have you determined what you will do if the opposition press the question?"

"I think I shall dodge it. I can take the ground that mine is simply an executive office, and it is not my province to make laws."

"That 's the doctrine, Governor."

"I think so. It 's the only safe ground for me to occupy in this canvass."

"It will take you through all right, Governor."

"I hope so. But we must get through with our business. It 's almost eleven."

"Here is the petition."

"How long have they been in prison?"

"About seven months."

"What is their sentence?"

"The Deacon's is seven years and Elijah's four."

"They must stay a while longer, Esquire. It will never do to pardon them so soon."

"Seven months, in the penitentiary, is a long time, Governor."

"So it is; but we are on the eve of an election, and the papers have made a great fuss about what they are pleased to term the abuse of the pardoning power."

"The election will be over in three weeks. Can I give them the assurance that they will be pardoned as soon as you have time to examine the papers?"

"I want to oblige you, Esquire; but the newspapers will give me a fearful lashing if I pardon them so soon."

"There are no papers in Elton."

"I know it; but there are a great many in the immediate vicinity."

"Not many."

"There are two at Glenville, two at Selridge, one at Melton, and one at Berwick."

"They are all in Jim Wells' district, and I will get the publishers to sign this petition. That will spike their guns."

"Can you get the opposition publishers to sign it?"

"I think I can. They are all very friendly to

14

Jim, and I will work up a sympathy for Mrs. Wells that will induce them to sign it."

"Newspaper publishers are not the most sympathetic men in the world."

"They are all right outside of politics, Governor; and if you'll agree to pardon my clients immediately after the election on condition that I get the signatures of the publishers to this petition, I will rest easy."

"All right.   I'll do it."

"Good bye, Governor."

"Good bye, Mr. Gray. Keep up my end of the string in Elton."

"We'll give you a majority that will make you feel proud of us, Governor."

"Well, 'Squire, did you see the Gov'ner?"

"Yes, sir."

"Have you got our pardon in your pocket?"

"No, Deacon; but I think I'm in a fair way to get it.   I'm bringing all the influences that I can command to bear on the Governor. The papers have been pitching into him for abusing the pardoning power, lately, and I must get the newspaper men of Glenville, Selridge, Melton, and Berwick to sign your petition in order to stop their clack."

" S'posin' they won't do it?"

" Then I can't get you pardoned."

" Seems to me 't is a queer noshun for a feller's pardon to depend on them newspaper chaps."

" There 's where it hinges. How many of the papers did you take?"

" I did n't take none of 'em. Me and Elijah do n't b'leve in newspapers, and Jim and Patience used to borry their 'n."

"Are you acquainted with any of the editors?"

" I know the edytur of the Glenville *Banner.* Me and him had a spat after Jim was nominated for a Congressman. He 's a little mite of a cuss with a big forrid, and sassyer 'n blazers."

" I 'll have a hard time of it with him, Deacon."

" Do n't tell him the petishun is for me, 'Squire. Git him to sign it without lookin' at it."

" Editors do n't sign papers that way, Deacon. He 's a great friend of Jim's. Perhaps I can get him to sign it for that reason."

"Do n't let Jim know what you 're up to, or he 'll spile your little game, 'Squire."

"I 'll keep mum so far as he 's concerned, Elijah."

"For my part I ain't a carin' wether they sign the petishun or not. If they do n't, we 'll save the land, and if I 's dad I 'd stick it out afore I 'd pay such a dredful price to git out o' here. You ask a good deal more 'n 't is wuth to do the work, 'Squire."

"You have no adequate idea of the magnitude of the undertaking, Elijah."

"Hain't no what?"

"No idea of the work."

"That 's right. Put it in English and I can understand what you 're talkin' about; but I could do the work in a week and cut the fire wood in the bargin."

"You could n't do it in a life-time, Elijah."

"If it wan't for dad you would n't git the job, 'Squire. How much of the timber land will you take to git dad out and let me stay?"

"It is the same labor to get one out as both."

"I do n't see how that comes."

"That 's because you do n't understand it."

"The papers is signed, Elijah, and 't is too late to make a fuss about it now."

"I s'pose 't is, father, but it 's a orful shame to let that timber priv'lege go."

"I know 't is, but it can't be helped. I 'll make Jack Blunt smart for it when I git out."

"You 'll have to catch him first, Deacon. He 's gone back to the Provinces."

"I know jest where to look for him, 'Squire."

"Well, good day, Deacon. I must go. 'T is almost train time."

"How long afore you 'll git us out?"

"It will take me a week to get the additional signatures. I will then forward the papers, and your pardon will probably come as soon as the Governor can find time to examine them."

"'T won't take him long to examine 'em, will it?"

"I hope not; but the campaign takes most of his time, now-a-days."

"Tell him he 'll git two more votes if he gits me and Elijah out before the elekshun. That 'll hurry him up."

"All right. I 'll tell him. Have you any word to send to your wife?"

"Yes. Tell her she'd better not sell no more butter now. If she'll put it down in pickle she'll git a bigger price for it in the winter."

"I suppose you know she has shut up the house and gone to live with Jim?"

"Shot up the house! No. I did n't know it. I'll make her smart for it when I git out. What's she done with the critters?"

"I do n't know."

"What's she done with the hens, 'Squire?"

"I do n't know."

"If them hens is gone I'll raise a rumpus when I git home."

"Find out what she's done with everything and send me a letter about it, 'Squire."

"All right, Deacon. I'll find out if I can."

"If you can't find the hens, go over to Phil Craig's. He's been tryin' to buy 'em of me for more 'n a year, and I'll bait he's got 'em."

"All right. I'll see him."

———

Esquire Gray found the newspaper publishers more "sympathetic" than the Governor predicted, and had no difficulty in procuring their names. In due time the petition was forwarded, and the pardon anxiously awaited. The election passed, the Governor was successful, and Esquire Gray — after waiting two weeks — grew impatient. He wrote to the Governor, reminding him of his promise. In a few days he received an answer. The petition "would be examined immediately." Without further delay the necessary papers were sent to the Prison Warden at Thomaston, and Hezekiah and Elijah Wells were free. The pardoning power was grossly abused by a man whom no one dared to approach with money; yet he was bribed by the promise of political preferment — an influence more subtle and far more potent than gold.

(By a recent act of the Legislature of Maine the pardoning power is withheld, and the ends of justice can no longer be subverted by political demagogues.)

Deacon Wells and his son returned to Elton without delay. Patience, contrary to the wishes of James, returned to her former home and took upon herself the burdens of her old life. The Deacon and Elijah were more cruel than ever, and the suffering wife and mother silently submitted, hoping that death would soon deliver her from a voluntary bondage; but the Angel of Death heeded not her prayer. Cruel and relentless, he comes not at the bidding of the weary and worn. He lingers on the threshold, unmindful of the tired heart's anguish, and heeds not the cry of the soul-sick sojourner, who fain would plunge into the noiseless, fathomless river.

CHAPTER X.

DIVORCED.

CALL the poor man back, Deacon. It is cruel to turn him from your door on such a bitter night."

"Do n't call me deacon no more, Patience. They 've turned me out o' church for nothin', and I won't be deaconed by nobody."

"I 'll call you anything you wish me to; but please do n't let that poor man perish in the cold. Will you call him back? "

"No. I 'll be — blowed if I do. He need n't freeze if he do n't want to. There 's other houses in Elton, and he can git into 'em."

"It is late, and most of our neighbors are in bed. If the poor man should freeze to death his blood would be on our hands, Dea—Hezekiah."

"I 'm boss of my own house, Patience, and that fellow can't stay here to-night if he does freeze; so that 's the end of it."

"I know this is your house, Hezekiah; but God will deal with us as we deal with His children."

"I do n't want none of your preachin', Patience.　I 'll be ——"

Patience Wells left the room.　She could not remain and listen to his profanity — one of his early habits revived at Thomaston, notwithstanding the salutary influence of the prison chaplain.

The following evening Elijah, almost breathless, entered the sitting room.

"Father, who 'd you s'pose you turned out doors last night?"

"I do n't know.　Some vagabone."

"No 'twan't.　'Twas Uncle George, from Novy Skoshy."

"How do you know?"

"I heerd it at the shoe shop when I 'se in to git my boots tapped."

"Where did he go to?"

"Up to Jim's.　They say he 's got a pile, and the boys was laffin' at me 'cause you would n't let him stay all night."

"Yes, and he 'll leave it all to Jim, now.

There's more of your work, Patience. You're allers spilin' my luck."

"Why, Hezekiah! I wanted you to let him in."

"But you ain't got sprawl enough to take care of folks when I do let 'em in. That's why I didn't let him stay."

"I have always endeavored to entertain your friends, Hezekiah."

"You're allers snivlin' round the house, and I'm 'shamed to ask nobody to come."

"I try to appear cheerful in presence of your company."

"You orter be allers cheerful and thankful to boot, Patience. You's nothin' but a poor orfin when I marrid you. If it hadn't been for me you wouldn't had no home."

"I'll admit that I married you for a home, Mr. Wells, and I have paid the penalty of my folly. I have been your slave and you have been a cruel master. This house is to me simply an abiding place, a shelter from the storm. It is not home. Through all the wearisome years that I have borne your name, you have not given me a kind word or a smile. Better, a thousand times better, a homeless orphan than an unloved wife. Heaven pity the poor girl that marries for a home."

"Then you marrid me for my money? It's preshus little of it you'll git if I do die fust. I've made my will."

"I don't want any of your money, Mr. Wells."

"What do you want?"

"Nothing but rest."

"I s'pose you want me to hire a gal and let you go gaddin' 'round among the neighbors?"

"That's jest what she wants, father. She's been up to Jim's 'til she's got spiled."

"And I wish you'd stayed up to Jim's, Patience. I don't want you snivlin' 'round here."

"I will go to-morrow."

"I'm glad you have come, mother. I've been very lonely without you. The house has not seemed like home since you left. You shall be tenderly cared for, and we will be so happy together."

"I cannot be happy, James. I am grateful

for your kindness, and your house shall be my refuge while I 'm waiting."

" You *shall* be happy, dear mother; and God grant that you may wait for many, many years."

" What have I to wait for, James? "

" You have me, mother."

" So I have, my dear boy; and you are very near to me; but I am so tired. I have waited so long for the summons, that life seems almost interminable. When the body is bent by age, and the heart withered by neglect, the tired soul must rest."

" You shall find rest here, dear mother; rest for your body and rest for your soul. You have broken the chain that bound you to a cruel, exacting husband, and you will enjoy your freedom. You must petition, at once, for a divorce."

For an instant a glad light beamed from the hazel eyes of Patience Wells. Could she, indeed, be free? Could she sever the chains that bound her, body and soul, to a man whom she utterly despised? Could she walk forth from the shadowy depths into the broad, full light of a new life? The thought was Heaven to her; but it was too bright, too gladdening to dwell in

the heart of Patience Wells. The prejudice of
her early training bound her still. She could
not hush the warning voice of a conscience that
had, in early life, been committed to the keeping
of " blind leaders of the blind."

" I cannot petition for a divorce, James."

" Why not?"

"Because it is wrong. It is contrary to the
teachings of the Bible, which is the rule and
guide of Faith."

" It is contrary to the teachings of men who
blindly endeavor to expound God's law, mother.
You are already divorced in spirit. Why should
you be bound in law?"

" Were there no other motive to restrain me,
I should shrink from the publicity of such a
proceeding, as much on your account as on my
own. Why urge me to plunge you into deeper
disgrace? Are not the crimes of your father
and brother enough?"

" A legal severance of the ties that bind you
to Hezekiah Wells would not disgrace either of
us, mother. God never joined you together.
Why should not man put asunder those whom
God hath not joined? You were cruelly de-

ceived, and your marriage has brought you only sorrow and pain."

"Let me suffer in silence a little longer, my dear boy. Death will soon divorce us."

"It shall not be, dear mother. Free from the vows that bind you to an unnatural husband, you will live many years to brighten my home."

"You are young and hopeful, James; but you are not a skillful artist. You paint a bright picture, leaving out the shadow in the background."

"But you are not old, dear mother. In the pure atmosphere of a happy home you shall look in vain for the shadow in the background of my picture. We will go out into the great world and enjoy the beautiful things that God has so lavishly given. Your last days shall be the brightest and happiest of your life."

"Do not tempt me to do violence to my conscience, James. Wait 'til I ask God about it."

"I will wait, dear mother, for I know that He will guide you aright."

"'Squire, I want a divorce from the old woman. Can you git it for me?"

"I presume so."

"What 'll you tax me for it?"

"About a hundred dollars."

"It 's too much.　You orter do it for fifty."

"Well, Deacon, as you 're an old client we won't fall out about the price.　What are your grounds for asking a divorce?"

"Patience is allers interferin' with my plans, and goes snivlin' 'round the house every time I make a good bargin and wants me to swap back."

"That is not sufficient ground for a divorce, Deacon."

"Must a man be allers tied to a woman that interferes when he 's makin' money accordin' to law?"

"The Court will require stronger ground than that, Deacon.　Has she failed in any of her wifely duties?"

"She has left my bed and board, but the bed was the one she brought with her when we was marrid."

"Where is she?"

"She 's up to Jim's."

"How did she go?　Did she leave you voluntarily?"

"She went afoot."

"Did you tell her to leave?"

The Deacon hesitated. Should he deceive his attorney? The thought flashed across his mind that Elijah could testify, and he answered :

"No, 'Squire. She left her own self."

"Then you can get a divorce."

"And you'll do it for fifty dollars?"

"Yes. Seeing it's you."

"I did think I'd never have nothin' more to do with you, 'Squire, 'cause you taxed me so steep for that prison bizness; but it comes sort o' nateral to come to you, and if you'll work cheaper in the futer I'll keep comin' right along."

"We won't quarrel about prices, Deacon."

"I don't want to quarrel with nobody, 'Squire, and when I git seprated from Patience I'll live pecerble the rest of my days."

"That's the way to live, Deacon. 'Live peaceably and die happy,' is a good motto."

"But I'm too young to think about dyin', 'Squire."

"It is said that 'the good die young,' but

15

that need not prevent you from reaching four
score, Deacon."

"Yes; and maybe more. I belong to a long
livin' fam'ly, and I may live to see seventy-
five."

"What will you do when you grow old,
Deacon?"

"I s'pose I'll set in a corner and chaw terbacker, like the rest of the old men."

"You'll have enough to keep you in good
style."

"Yes; I'll have a purty fair nest-aig, but I
do n't want no style about me. I b'leve in livin'
plain like, and that's one thing I've got agin
Patience. She wants to be too primp."

"Can you prove that she's been extravagant
and wasteful?"

"I'll have to have a witness to prove that;
won't I, 'Squire?"

"Yes, sir."

"Well; I can prove it by Elijah. He's a
witness."

"Yes. He'll do."

"And I can prove that she fed good soap

grease to the hens, and used aigs instead of codfish skin to settle coffee when she had company."

" What did she use to settle coffee when she had no company?"

" She did n't make no coffee, them times."

" Then she is not very extravagant."

" Yes she is. She'd a made it if I'd let her."

" Did she make tea?"

" No, sir."

" What did you drink?"

" Sweetened water and buttermilk."

" Did she make a great deal of pastry?"

" Make what? "

" Pies, tarts, cake, etc."

" No, sir."

" What did she cook?"

" Fried mush and codfish hash."

" I will not allege that she was wasteful or extravagant. I will put it on the ground of abandonment."

" I do n't care what grounds you put it on; but Elijah will swear that she's orful wasting, if you want him to."

"I do n't think I want him to, Deacon. I 'll file the papers at once."

"All right, 'Squire. Make 'em strong."

"I will."

———

"God has answered your prayer, dear mother. Father has commenced proceedings for a divorce."

"Who told you?"

"I was in the Clerk's office at Glenville, to-day, when the papers were filed."

"What shall I do about it?"

"I shall see Mr. Ainsworth as soon as the notice is served on you, and ask him to file a cross bill."

"You know best, James, and I shall place the matter in your hands."

"All right, mother. It shall be so managed as to give you but little trouble."

"Will I have to go to Court?"

"Yes. We will need you."

"Is there no way to avoid it?"

"No, mother. If we let the case go by default the record will show that you were wholly to blame. He has charged that you voluntarily abandoned him."

"I will go."

When the case of Hezekiah Wells *vs.* Patience Wells was called, Mr. Ainsworth appeared for the defendant and filed a cross bill, setting forth the many acts of cruelty of which the plaintiff was guilty; praying that a divorce, together with alimony, be granted to the defendant. The Court granted the prayer of Patience Wells, and decreed that Hezekiah Wells should pay her the sum of forty thousand dollars, in semi-annual payments of five thousand dollars, with six per cent. interest from the date of the decree.

When the judgment of the Court was announced, Deacon Wells was thunderstruck. He told the Judge he 'd "ruther live with Patience than pay her more 'n five hundred dollars," and he "guessed he 'd dismiss the case and let him take the divorce back." He thought it "a strange proceedin'" when the Court informed him that the matter had passed beyond his control.

" It 's orful, Elijah."

" Shure 's you 're born."

" Thirty thousand to git out o' prison and forty thousand to git red of a wife, all in one year."

" Yes; and I 'm the wust loser by it."

" You' re the only loser, Elijah. There 's enough left to last me my life time."

" And they say Jim 's wuth fifty thousand dollars, and still a makin' of it; and he 'll git all this forty thousand."

" Yes; Patience 'll give it all to him."

" Shure 's you 're born."

" If we can lose seventy thousand dollars in a year, how long will it take to lose a hundred thousand, Elijah?"

" I do n't know."

" You orter know. You studied 'rithmetick in skule."

" But that 's a sum in desolate frackshuns, and I 've forgot 'em."

" You orter remember your skulin', Elijah. You may have to depend on it for a livin' if things keep goin' this way."

" I 'll never teech skule for a livin' as long

as there's any yearlins in the country for sale."

"It'll keep us humpin' to make them semmy aneral payments, Elijah."

"What is semmy aneral payments, father?"

"Once in two years, Elijah. It's strange how fast you're forgittin' your jografy."

CHAPTER XI.

ON'T you want to take a ride with me, to-day, Uncle George?"

"I shall be pleased to go, James. 'T is a delightful morning and I always enjoy a sleighride."

"All right. I shall be ready in an hour. In the mean time you can have a chat with mother."

"Go and attend to your business, James. Do n't worry about me. I am enjoying my visit so much that I fear I shall protract it beyond the allotted time."

George Wells, as the reader has already divined, is wholly unlike Hezekiah. They were as widely different in their youth as in their manhood. George was studious, industrious, and upright, while Hezekiah was thoughtless, lazy, and dishonest. While George was at school, Hezekiah was robbing bird's nests or indulging in cock-fighting. His associates were idle and dissolute, and he went on from bad to worse until, at the age of twenty-two, he was compelled to leave home, or suffer the penalty of the offended law. He fled to Calais, where he engaged in smuggling. His operations were successful, and during a period of three years he accumulated several thousand dollars. Stimulated by good fortune, he openly violated the revenue laws until the officers tracked him, when he fled to Elton, and joined the church in order to conceal his true character and continue his smuggling operations without fear of detection.

George, in the mean time, was steadily working his way up in the world. He had acquired a fair English education, and was blessed with a liberal share of common sense. He engaged in shipping land plaster to Boston and Philadelphia, and soon became one of the heaviest operators in the Province. After Hezekiah left Calais he heard nothing from him. No letters passed between them. The Deacon heard, through Jack Blunt, that "George was shippin' plaster, and was wuth more 'n a hundred thousand dollars," but Jack did not make himself known to George. The Deacon was surprised to learn that George had accumulated a fortune by fair dealing, and had Jack reported the sum correctly his surprise would have been still greater. He did not dream that honest toil would bring a rich reward. According to his idea, fraud was the only road to wealth.

A personal notice of "Congressman Wells," in a Boston paper, attracted George's attention, and he read it with deep interest. He learned that James Wells was the son of a Nova Scotian, and that his home was in Elton. The name was not common in Nova Scotia, and he surmised that James Wells was his nephew. James was a prominent member of Congress, and George fondly hoped that Hezekiah had reformed. Seized by an irresistible desire to see his brother, he went home and made his arrangements to visit Elton. At Berwick he found the coach crowded, and was compelled to ride on the outside with the driver. This arrangement was satisfactory, notwithstanding the bitter cold, as it would afford him an opportunity to learn something of James Wells and his family. He gave the driver a "pure Havana," and opened the conversation.

"Do you know a man named Wells, in Elton?"

"Oh, yes. Everybody on this route knows Deacon Wells."

"What's his given name?"

"Hezekiah."

"Do you know where he came from?"

"Yes, sir; he's from Novy Skoshy."

"What kind of a man is he?"

"He's a hard ticket, sir. I guess them Novy Skoshyans is all hard tickets. Leastwise, he and Jack Blunt is. The Deacon has been in the penitenshary, and Jack orter be."

"What was the Deacon sent for?"

"He and Lige, his oldest boy, was sent for forgin' a deed. The old Deacon got seven years and Lige four."

"When were they sentenced?"

"About a year ago. They only had to stay seven or eight months. The Govner pardoned 'em out three or four months ago."

"Then James Wells, the Congressman, is not the Deacon's son?"

"Yes he is; but he's no more like him than I'm like a full-feathered angel. Jim's the best feller in Ameriky, and jest as smart as a steel trap. God has quit makin' better men than Jim Wells, and I'm doubtin' if He ever commenced makin' 'em."

"How does it come that there is such a wide difference between him and Elijah?"

"Why, you see, the Lord made Jim and the devil made Lige. That's my idee about it, but most folks say it's inherited by Jim and Lige from their father and mother. The Deacon marrid one of the best wimmin that was ever crowded into shoe leather, and Jim's jest like her in looks and actions, while Lige is as much like his father as the telegraph is like a streak of lightnin'. It's sort o' puzzlin' how they come so."

"Why is Hezekiah called Deacon?"

"He was a reg'lar blood and thunder deacon 'til he got into the penitenshary. He jined church to help him in his rum smugglin' bizness, and he looked so confounded meek and innersent that they soon made a deacon of him; but he's jest about as fit for a deacon as I am for a minister. His heart's harder 'n the devil's off horn, and he's got no more religion than a yaller jacket."

"How many children has he?"

"Only Jim and Lige."

"Are they married?"

"No. Jim's got a big house, but he ain't marrid, and there ain't a gal in Elton mean enough to marry Lige."

"Where does Hezekiah live?"

"In a big brown house on the east side of the road, jest above the church."

"Does he live in good style?"

"I guess he do n't put on no scollops sense he got out of prison, and he's too stingy to eat anything but codfish hash. I never eat a meal in his house, but they say he lives so cheap that the flies all starve to death, and a church mouse could n't stan' it a week."

"I am much obliged for your information."

"You're intirely welcome, sir. It's a driver's duty to tell a passenger everything he knows, and some of 'em tell an orful sight more, 'though the drivers on this route is a purty fair set, considerin' their ockerpashun."

"Stage drivers are generally truthful, are they not?"

"Not so orful. They see a good many gentlemen and a good many shams. 'T ain't often we git a geniwine Seth Thomas Havana weed like this. They give us a penny grab and smoke the good ones theirselves. It's the shams that makes the drivers lie."

"It takes all kinds of people to make a world, you know."

"Yes, sir; but a stage driver's world is made up mostly of one kind, and I'm sorry to say they are not like you, sir. We only know there's big fish 'cause we see the little ones."

"I do n't understand your reasoning."

"If there was n't no big fish to eat the shrimps, it stands to reason that the shrimps would n't a been created, and the little men that ride with us was created for somethin'."

"I suppose nothing was created in vain."

"Maybe not; but I guess 't would puzzle the wise men of Boston to tell what Canady thistles was created for, onless 't was to keep boys from goin' barefoot. I do n't believe they was made 'til after shoemakin' was invented."

"Then you do n't like Canada thistles?"

"No, sir. I lost my appertite for 'em when I was a little boy."

"Were you raised on a farm?"

"I was n't exactly raised anywhere. I kind o' growed up 'twixt a farm and a saw-mill, and then went to stage drivin' on this route."

"How long have you been driving?"

"Ever sense I's born, almost; but accordin' to the way my present father sot my age down in the famly Bible, I was born at fourteen, and I 've been drivin' stage ever sense."

"Do you like it?"

"Not so overly much; but it beats nothin' all holler. If it 's true that this life is the end of a man, I might as well die drivin' stage as anything else."

"But this life is not the end. There is a life beyond the grave."

"Maybe there is. I 'm not prepared to deny it; but they 've argued the question on this route 'til I 've got all mixed up about it. I took a little feller with a wite choker down one trip, and he told me he had a shure thing on goin' to Heaven. The next trip up I took him to Glenville for stealin' hosses, and the Sheriff said he had a shure thing on goin' to the penitenshary. And that's the way it goes with stage drivers. They hain't got no shure thing on nothin' but a hard life and poor pay. Here's Elton, sir. Where shall I set you down?"

"At the hotel, if you please."

"'Tain't much of a hotel. 'Tis only a country tavern, and a poor one at that."

"It will not be my first night in a country tavern, my friend."

"Tell 'em to give you lots of bed close to-night. There's a big storm a brewin', and it's goin' to be a screamer."

"Thank you. I'll tell them."

"Here we are. Run right in. I'll bring your trunk."

The driver deposited the heavy trunk in the bar-room. George gave him a dollar and two more Havanas. He was profuse in his thanks, and mounted the box apparently unmindful of the bitter cold. "He's a geniwine gentleman, and no mistake. There's no rancid cod-liver ile about him. He's sound to the core, and knows jest how to treat a whip. Git up, boys. It's goin' to be colder 'n a Glenville prayer meetin' afore you git there."

George Wells was greatly depressed by the stage driver's account of Hezekiah's criminal conduct. He was tempted to return to his home without making himself known to his relatives, but he yielded to a natural desire to see his brother, and started out in the dark. As he approached the house he determined to apply for shelter from the furious storm. The reader knows the result. George went back to the hotel and spent a sleepless night. He had been turned from the door of his only brother in a manner that convinced him of that brother's utter heartlessness.

The next morning he called on James, who gave him a welcome that induced him to protract his visit. James enjoyed his uncle's society, and the attachment was mutual. He managed to spend many of his evenings at home with his mother and "Uncle George," who joined him in urging Patience to apply for a divorce. It was not strange that George

16

should be irresistibly drawn toward James and Patience. They were all the world to him, for all his relatives were in Elton. He avoided Hezekiah and Elijah, and was content with James, Patience, and his books.

At the appointed time James drove up to the door.

"All ready, Uncle?"

"All ready, James."

"Where shall we drive?"

"Anywhere. Your company and the ride is what I want."

"I have a young friend, about twelve miles from here, whom I think you will like. He lives on the Berwick road, and it is a pleasant drive. Shall we go there?"

"I shall be pleased to meet any of your friends."

"You will like Harry Jones. He is crippled, and is necessarily confined to the house; but he is a good conversationist, and you will be surprised at his thorough knowledge of the world."

"Was he born a cripple?"

"Yes, sir."

"Then he owes his knowledge of the world to books?"

"And newspapers."

"It is difficult to determine which are the best educators."

"We could not get along without both; yet I should give newspapers the preference."

"We differ on that point, James. Books contain all that is worth preserving."

"By no means, Uncle. It is simply a more convenient form of preserving important facts. The Press has made rapid strides in the past twenty years, and the newspaper gives us not only the current events of the day, but a concise history of the past. It treats of scientific subjects and presents them in the most pleasing form. The man who confines himself to books, knows comparatively little of the great world in which he lives. The newspaper of to-day is the foundation for many books. It is the source of the book-writer's information."

"But newspapers contain so much that is pernicious."

"The same is true of books. We have the

good and the bad in both, but the good predominates."

"How is it with the great human family, James? Does the good predominate?"

"I think it does. I have seen more good than evil in the world."

"That is not the prevailing opinion. Your experience is widely at variance with many close observers."

"That is because they shut their eyes to the good, and see only the evil that is in the world. They are not impartial observers."

"There is so much crime in the world, James. Murder and theft are of daily occurrence, and the social evil is alarming in its extent and rapid growth."

"I believe that nine of every ten men are honest, and ninety-nine of every hundred women are virtuous, Uncle. One rascal will make more noise in the world than a dozen honest men."

"I hope you will never have occasion to change your mind, James. It is best to look on the bright side."

" And there is a bright side to every real picture."

" But it is not always visible, James. Some people are so constituted that they can't see the bright things in the world."

" They are not ' real folks,' Uncle. Only the visionary spend their lives in mourning over fancied grievances."

" Acute pain is born of imaginary ills, and the real is no worse than the seeming. Look at the vast number of people who have the ' blues ' without a cause. Are they not deserving of sympathy?"

"Certainly they are; but they are not practical people. No man with a well-balanced mind will be ' blue ' without a cause. ' Blues ' is simply another name for mild insanity."

" Then the world is only an asylum for the insane."

" By no means. The great majority of mankind are not troubled with the ' blues.' It is usually inherited, and should be treated as other diseases of the mind."

" What is your prescription, James?"

" I am not a physician, Uncle, but I derived

great benefit from the stereotyped prescription: Hard work, pleasant companions, pure air, and wholesome food."

" Then you have had the blues? "

" Yes, sir; but I have entirely recovered."

" I have taken your prescription for years, with the exception of the pleasant companions, and have found no relief."

" You have omitted an important ingredient. Add the 'pleasant companions' and I will guarantee a permanent cure."

" Thank you. I will act on your suggestion. I am satisfied that I have lived too much alone."

" It seems so strange that you never married, Uncle."

" My bride is in Heaven, James. She went home two weeks before the day appointed for our wedding. Sometimes, when I am very, very lonely, I go and sit beside her grave and imagine that I feel her presence. It may be only seeming, but the solace is real. It has robbed death of its sting and the grave of its terrors. The hope that we may be united has been the one great comfort of my life. When I would sin, her gentle influence restrains me. When I would die, she bids me live. She guides me now as in the long ago, when her pure life and kindly teachings revealed the glories of a blessed immortality."

For a time, both were silent; both were thinking. They were trying to solve the mystery of our being. George was first in giving utterance to his thoughts, and a long discussion on the subject of spiritualism followed. A subject nearest the heart and farthest from the brain; a theme that man cannot grasp, and upon which the angels are silent.

Bessie Jones was spending a week with Harry while the school house at Elton was being repaired. Although no longer compelled to work, she could not remain idle, and her attachment for her old pupils induced her to teach another term. James introduced his uncle, and a few hours were spent in pleasant and profitable conversation. George was so well pleased with Harry and Bessie that he asked James to drive down again during the week — a proposition that was gladly accepted. At four o'clock they started for home.

" You didn't speak of the young lady on the

way down, James. She seems as much your friend as Harry."

" I think I did n't mention her name. We were talking so steadily about other subjects that I forgot to speak of her. She is a very dear friend. What do you think of her?"

" She is an intelligent, sensible, womanly woman, James. I like her very much."

" So do I. We agree on that point, Uncle. I hope the day is not far distant when she will be more to me than a dear friend."

" Such a union cannot be otherwise than happy, my dear nephew, and I hope you will be abundantly blessed."

" Thank you."

" I thought she was more than a friend, James. I noticed that she blushed deeply when that old lady asked when you would want the little stockings."

" You will have to visit Bessie and Harry without me, to-day, Uncle."

" Why so?"

" I have just received a dispatch from Mr.

Ainsworth, stating that an important case in which we are interested will be called for trial to-morrow."

"Can't you get back in time to take the evening stage?"

"I am going. up with Mr. Lamb. We will start in about an hour. You can drive the blacks without trouble, if you 'll hold them back a little on the start."

"I am not much of a horseman; but I can either manage them or accept the alternative, and let them run."

"Here they are. I will see if John has everything all right."

"I 'll risk John. He is very careful."

"All right, Uncle. Jump in."

George took the reins, and the blacks started off in a brisk trot. As they descended the hill, near Mrs. Love's, they began to run, and soon became unmanageable. George tried in vain to check their speed. At the foot of the hill a yoke of oxen were plodding along with a heavily loaded sled. The danger of a collision was imminent. George could not turn the horses from the road and the oxen could not get out of the way. Robbie Bently, who was walking up the hill, took in the situation at a glance, and resolved to stop the horses, if possible. On the opposite side of the road was a deep snow-drift. If he could frighten them into the drift they could be easily checked. He stood very near the road until they were almost upon him, when he suddenly opened his umbrella. The startled horses plunged into the deep snow and were soon stopped.

"Thank you, my little man. That was bravely done."

"You 're welcome, sir. Is anything broke?"

"I believe not."

Robbie waited until George quieted the horses by patting their necks, when he started up the hill.

"Hold on, my brave fellow. Here 's a little spending money for you."

"Thank you. I do n't want any money, sir."

"But you must take it. I shall not feel right unless you do."

"This is too much, sir. It 's a ten-dollar bill."

"I know it. I think 't is a cheap runaway, too. What is your name?"

"It used to be Robbie Bently; but they call me Ragged Bob since I'm only a bound boy. They don't call me that as much as they used to, 'though, since Bessie Jones give me this coat."

"Then Bessie Jones is a good friend, is she?"

"Yes, sir. She's good to everybody, 'cause she can't help it. I guess God made her so."

"How did you happen to have an umbrella this bright morning?"

"Mr. Lee, the man I live with, borrowed it last night, and I was jest taking it home to Mrs. Love's."

"It is fortunate for me that he borrowed it. Does Mr. Lee treat you kindly?"

"I s'pose he treats me as well as bound boys are generally treated. 'T ain't like livin' at home, you know."

"Are your parents dead?"

"Yes, sir. My father died when I was a little boy. We lived on the place 'til Deacon Wells bought it and turned us out; then mother died, and we children were bound out."

"Did Deacon Wells buy the place of your mother?"

"No, sir. He bought it of the Sheriff. Father owed a thousand dollars, and the place had to go to pay it."

"What is the place worth?"

"About three thousand dollars."

"And Deacon Wells bought it for a thousand?"

"Yes, sir."

"And turned your mother out of the house?"

"Yes, sir."

"Have you any brothers or sisters?"

"Yes, sir. I have two sisters living. Two of my sisters died last summer."

"Do they live in Elton?"

"No, sir. Susie lives at Berwick and Anna at Glenville. She's bound to the tavern keeper."

"Are they kindly treated?"

"'Bout like the common run of bound girls, I guess."

"Good morning, my boy. I'll see you again."

George Wells resolved to look after the Bently children. They had been wronged by his brother; but he would right that wrong, so far as money was concerned. He would refund the two thousand dollars, and see that it was wisely expended in educating the orphans.

———

"Good morning, Miss Jones."

"Good morning, Mr. Wells. I am glad to see you."

"Thank you. You see I have not brought my welcome with me. James was called to Glenville, this morning, and could not come."

"You are very welcome on your own account, Mr. Wells."

"I do n't doubt it; but we could have a very enjoyable day if James were here."

"We can have an enjoyable day without him."

"But it won't be quite so happy, Bessie."

"I do n't know how much you and Mr. Wells will miss him. I shall enjoy the day very much, Harry."

"So shall I, Bessie. I am going to be as happy as I can without James; but there is a world of sunshine in his bright eyes, and we shall all miss him."

,"He 's a royal good fellow, Mr. Jones, and it is not strange that you should like him."

"He has been very good to us, and we appreciate his kindness. He often gives me a ride behind his beautiful blacks."

"The blacks ran away with me, this morning."

"How did you stop them?"

"Robbie Bently frightened them into a snow drift."

"That 's an odd way to stop a runaway team."

"But it is a very sure way, Miss Jones, when the snow is deep enough."

"How did he frighten them?"

"He stood beside the road and frightened them by suddenly spreading his umbrella. He was remarkably cool about it."

"Robbie is a remarkable boy, Mr. Wells. His opportunities have not been good, but he has improved wonderfully in two years. He is one of my best pupils, and I am anxious to see him succeed. If he could have the privilege of going to school he would learn rapidly. He is kept at home every other day, and yet he keeps up with his class."

"If he was a little further advanced I should like to take him home with me. I need a faithful boy."

"What do you want him to do?"

"Keep books and attend to my correspondence."

"If you will take him one year from now, I will guarantee that he shall be qualified. I will teach him book-keeping this winter, and will work very hard to make him all that you desire, so far as it is in my power to do so. I think I can teach him grammar, penmanship and punctuation during the winter evenings. I will ask Mr. Lee to let him come to Mrs. Love's, where I can devote much time to him. Pardon me for asking so much. I feel a deep interest in Robbie's welfare."

"I am glad the poor boy has so true a friend, Miss Jones."

"He is truthful, intelligent and kind-hearted, Mr. Wells. He is worthy of my friendship. You are aware that he is not educated, if you have talked with him; but a little schooling has wrought such a change that I feel confident that he will soon learn what you require; and I know you can trust him."

"It shall be as you suggest, Miss Jones. I will take him next winter, if our lives be spared; provided, always, that he will come to me."

"Thank you, Mr. Wells. He will cheerfully go to you. He is so anxious to do something to help his sisters."

"Will Mr. Lee let him go?"

"Oh, yes. He says Robbie is a burden to him. He will gladly let him go."

"I will call on Mr. Lee, when I return, and arrange the matter."

"I am so glad. Poor Robbie has had a hard life, of late, and the change will be very agreeable to him."

"Is Mr. Lee unkind to him?"

"I do n't know that he is positively unkind; but he is rather frugal, and Robbie works very hard. Mr. Lee tells him that he does not earn the bread he eats, and that is not consoling, you know."

"No; it is n't very comforting. We will put

Robbie in a place where he can earn his bread, if Mr. Lee will let us do it."

The day passed in pleasant conversation. Bessie and Harry persuaded Mr. Wells to remain until after tea, and it was past nine o'clock when he drove up to the stable door where John awaited him.

"Be sure to rub them well, John. We came along pretty lively."

"I'll take good care of the beauties, Mr. Wells. I believe in bein' kind to hosses. It's my religion."

"Your religion is good so far as it goes, John; but I hope it is not restricted to the horses."

"I'm no stricter with 'em than I orter be. They're the best span of hosses in Maine, and I'll look out for 'em as long as they're in my keepin', sir."

"All right, John. Here's half a dollar to pay you for waiting."

"Thank you, sir. I'd like to wait seven evenin's in a week on the same terms."

James was detained three days at Glenville. On his return, George made arrangements with him for educating the Bently girls. James

17

cheerfully accepted the trust, and added a thousand dollars to the fund set apart for that purpose.

"I shall provide for Robbie myself, James. Bessie Jones is going to teach him book-keeping this winter, and I will take him into my office next year."

"I 'm glad you feel an interest in his welfare. His father was an intelligent man, and Robbie closely resembles him. There is something in the boy, and, under proper influences, he will make more than an average man."

"Bessie Jones will make a man of him, James. She has planned for me, and I heartily indorse her scheme."

"I know she thinks a great deal of Robbie. She has spoken so favorably of him that I thought of putting him in my office if he wished it; but your plan is better."

"I must go and see Mr. Lee to-morrow, and get his consent. I called yesterday, but he was n't at home."

"Mr. Lee will not give him up without compensation."

"Bessie thinks he will gladly let him go."

"She does n't know him as well as I do."

"He says Robbie don't earn the bread he eats."

"That is his way of talking, Uncle. He is narrow and parsimonious. He will not consider the welfare of Robbie, but will measure the matter by the standard of dollars and cents."

"Then I must buy his consent with dollars and cents, James."

"I fear you will have to."

"Good morning, Mr. Lee. I came to see you in regard to Robbie Bently."

"Yes, sir. He lives with me. I suppose I shall have to look out for him until he is twenty-one, but he is a poor stick, and is quite a burden to me. I suppose you want to sell him a suit of clothes, but I can't afford to dress him any better. He 's got a good coat."

"I am not in the clothing business, Mr. Lee."

"I guess I 'm mistaken in the man. I took you for the Glenville tailor."

"My name is Wells. I live at Windsor, Nova Scotia, and I want to take Robbie Bently there next year.　He is a burden to you, and I'll take him off your hands if you'll let me."

"Yes; he's a burden; but I've got used to his ways, and I guess I'll keep him."

"He will suit me, Mr. Lee, and I'll do well by him if you'll let him go.　I want to put him in my office, and will pay him good wages.　You certainly want to see him get ahead in the world."

"Yes, sir; but I'm doing a good part by the boy.　I send him to school every other day, and let him sleep in the main part of the house."

"At twenty-one he will be turned out into the world without a trade or other means of earning a livelihood.　I will teach him how to conduct a lucrative business."

"I ain't very forehanded, Mr. Wells, and I can't afford to let Bob go.　I've taken care of him for two years, and he is getting big enough to earn his living, now."

"I will give you a hundred dollars if you will let him go next winter."

"I can't let him go for a hundred dollars, Mr. Wells.　He has three years to stay before he will be of age.　He is worth three hundred dollars a year to me. He's as good as a man, in haying time, and he plants potatoes, feeds the stock, cuts all my wood, helps my wife wash, and does a great many other things. 'T would cost me three hundred dollars a year to hire a man to fill his place."

"Then he is n't such a 'burden' to you, after all."

"He has been a burden, but he ain't now. He's money in my pocket, and I 'd be a fool to let him go."

"Then you do not consider how much he would be benefited by going with me?"

"No, sir. I am considering S. B. Lee's interest just now; not Robert Bently's."

"Is n't it your duty to help the boy? or, at least, to throw no obstacle in the way of those who are willing to help him?"

"I think it 's my duty to consult my own interest in the matter, sir. I presume you did not call to teach me my duty?"

"No, sir. I called for the purpose of aiding a poor, neglected orphan, and I am resolved to do it, either with or without your consent."

"How can you do it without my consent?

He was bound to me by a proper officer, and the contract is legal."

"Did it never occur to you that you were also bound by that contract, Mr. Lee?"

"Of course I am bound by it. I am bound to feed and clothe him, and I shall keep the contract."

"You have already violated it, Mr. Lee. You were bound to send him to school so many months in each year. This you have not done. Even the coat he wears was given him by a friend. His clothing has been scanty and ragged. Why is he called 'Ragged Bob?' Simply because you have violated your contract and have not dressed him decently. You knew he was friendless and have shamefully abused him; but he is friendless no longer and he shall be free from this bondage."

"What are you going to do about it?"

"I am going to see lawyer Ainsworth and have the contract annulled."

Mr. Lee was not prepared for this. He knew that he had broken the contract, and he felt guilty. There was something in George's manner that convinced the avaricious guardian that he was in earnest, and would take steps at once for the release of the bound boy.

"I don't believe you can have the contract annulled, for I have treated him as well as bound boys are usually treated; but I have no money to fool away in a law suit. I'll take the hundred dollars and let him go next winter after he gets the wood cut."

"And you are to let him go to school this winter, and to Mrs. Love's evenings to learn book-keeping of Miss Jones?"

"I'll let him go to school every other day; and I don't care where he goes evenings, after he gets his chores done."

"That won't do, Mr. Lee. He must go to school regularly this winter."

"Well; I suppose I'll have to let him go, but I can't spare him very well. I am feeding a good deal of stock this winter."

"And you must get him some good, warm clothing."

"All right."

"Here's your hundred dollars."

George wrote an article of agreement, which was signed by Mr. Lee, and took his departure.

He must see Robbie and get his consent to his plans. Thus far he and Bessie had proceeded without consulting the bound boy.

———

"And so you've been talking about me to Mr. Wells, have you? I've a notion to give you a good licking. young man."

"No, sir. I have n't."

"Do n't lie to me, Bob. How did he know you only went to school every other day; and how did he know that Bessie Jones gave you that coat?"

"I told him about Bessie giving me the coat; but I did n't talk about you."

"And you told him I abused you, and you wanted to leave me and go to Nova Scotia with him?"

"No, sir. He has n't said anything to me about going to Nova Scotia."

"Do you want to go?"

"Yes, sir. I should like to go if you will let me."

"Then you want to leave me?"

"Yes, sir."

"Why do you want to leave me, Bob?"

"Because it does n't seem like home to me here."

"Have I not treated you kindly?"

"No, sir. You are always finding fault with me, and telling me that I 'm a burden to you."

"And you told Mr. Wells so?"

"No, sir. I did n't."

"Then how did he find it out?"

"I do n't know. It 's common talk. The boys at school are always calling me 'Ragged Bob' and 'Lee's burden.' I suppose you talk to others the same as you do to me."

"Do you think you 'll fare any better with Mr. Wells than you do here?"

"Yes, sir. I think he will be kind to me."

"And these are the thanks I get for keeping an object of charity from the poor house."

"I am not an object of charity, Mr. Lee. I have worked very hard for you, and I know I have earned my board and clothing. Fred Ball gets twelve dollars a month for doing less work than I do for you, and you have never given me a dollar. I can't have a pair of skates, a hand-sled or any of the things that other boys have.

In the two years that I have lived with you I have n't had a cent until Mr. Wells gave me some for stopping his team when it was running away."

" How much did he give you?"

" Ten dollars."

" Ten dollars!　What have you done with it?"

" I 've got it laid away."

" Go and bring it to me."

" Oh, please, Mr. Lee, let me keep it.　I want to save it towards getting a plain stone for mother's grave."

" Bring it to me at once, I say.　Why did n't you tell me of it before?　It 's as bad as stealing to keep money secreted that belongs to me."

" It do n't belong to you, Mr. Lee.　Mr. Wells gave it to me."

" And you are a bound boy, and everything you earn belongs to me."

" I did n't earn it.　'T was a gift."

" All that is given to you is mine.　You 're a fine specimen to talk about buying tombstones. Bring me the money at once, and if you say a word about it to anybody, I 'll lick you within an inch of your life."

With tears of regret the bound boy gave up his treasure. And Mr. Lee walked forth into the bright, glad sunlight, and breathed the same pure air as those who wear more than the semblance of manhood.

CHAPTER XII.

ODDS AND ENDS.

ERE'S more trouble, Elijah."

"What's up now, father?"

"Harry Jones has brung a suit agin me for his intrust in the place."

"Who brung it for him?"

"Mr. King; that red-headed cuss that sent us to Thomaston. I've already paid forty-three thousand dollars for that infernal place."

"How do you make that out?"

"I paid five thousand in the fust place, did n't I?"

"Yes."

"Then I paid Bessie Jones eight thousand more, did n't I?"

"Yes."

"Then I paid 'Squire Gray thirty thousand to get us out of the penitenshary, did n't I?"

"Yes."

“Well, that makes forty-three thousand, don't it?”

“Shure's you're born.”

“Then I paid Jack Blunt and Tom Siddons fifty dollars for apprisin' it, did n't I?”

“Yes.”

“How much does that make, Elijah?”

“Wait 'till I git my slate.”

“You orter be able to do that sum in your head.”

“They did n't teach no mental 'rithmetick when I went to skule.”

“So they did n't. Skules has changed, like everything else.”

“Yes ; and, like everything else, they 've changed for the wus. Accordin' to skules now-a-days, I don't know nothin'.”

“You 'll never die of depreshun of the brain, Elijah.”

“No. If things keeps on I 'll die in the poor house.”

“So you will.”

“What are you goin' to do about Harry Jones, father?”

"I'm goin' to see 'Squire Gray. You may saddle up old Charley and I'll start."

"I'll have him ready in a minit."

———

"'Squire, Harry Jones is after me for his intrust in the place."

"What are you going to do about it, Deacon?"

"That's what I'm here to find out."

"I think you'd better compromise with him. He'll get Ainsworth to fight it for him, and you'll get whipped every time. Jack Blunt has been blowing about that appraisement."

"I wish I had him here. I'd make him smart for it."

"The mischief is done, and it's too late to talk about 'makin' him smart' now. You should have made him smart enough to keep his tongue still."

"What do you s'pose Harry'll charge me?"

"I don't know. Two or three thousand dollars, probably. Perhaps more."

"Yes; it will be shure to be more, 'Squire."

"Do you want me to go and see him?"

"I guess I'll go and see him myself. Maybe I can beat him down a little."

"All right, Deacon. You go and see him."

"Look a here, 'Squire; folks don't call me Deacon no more, and if it's all the same to you, I wish you'd quit it."

"It's all the same to me, Dea — Mr. Wells. I'll call you Mr. Wells after this."

"Or Hezekiah, which is all one to me."

"All right."

Hezekiah mounted old Charley and called on Harry Jones. He was referred to Mr. Ainsworth. He tried to settle the matter with Harry, but was informed that "Mr. Ainsworth knew all about it." He went back to Esquire Gray and reported the result of his interview.

"I think you had better go and see Ainsworth yourself, Mr. Wells."

"I don't want no dealin's with him, 'Squire. He's too sharp for me. I've tried him afore. If I go to him he'll rig a purchase to make me pay Harry Jones' lawyer's fee."

"Well; I'll go and see him to-morrow. What is the highest price I'm authorized to offer?"

"It's the lowest price I'm after, 'Squire.

You 're authorized to offer the lowest price that 'll bring it."

" Of course, I shall get it as low as I can; but suppose he should ask six thousand dollars?"

" Git it for five if you can, 'Squire."

" All right. I 'll do the best I can for you."

" Do n't offer more 'n three thousand on the start."

" I won't. How shall I fix the time of payment?"

" Make it in semmy anneral payments, 'Squire."

" That is rather short time, Mr. Wells. The first installment of your wife's alimony will be due in about four months, and you will have a great deal of money to raise."

" It ain't due for nigh onto two years, 'Squire. It 's in semmy anneral payments."

" Certainly. Five thousand every six months."

" No. Five thousand every two years."

" You 're mistaken, Mr. Wells. Semi-annual means half yearly. You will have to pay five thousand dollars every six months."

" Then I 'm ruined, 'Squire. I thought semmy anneral was every two years. I can't sell property fast enough to pay five thousand dollars every six months.”

“Perhaps you can get the time extended by paying eight or ten per cent. interest.”

“That will be orful, ’Squire. I ’m payin’ ten per cent. on the Bessie Jones morgidge, now, and I can’t stan’ no more ten per cents.”

“I supposed you understood the matter, or I should have asked the Court to extend the time. You made no objection then.”

“’Cause I s’posed it was once in two years. Can’t you ask the Court to give me more time?”

“It ’s too late now. The judgment has been entered on the record.”

“I can’t pay it. They ’ll have to take what little I ’ve got and send me to the poor house. You can tell ’em so, ’Squire, and maybe they ’ll give me more time.”

“I ’ll see Mr. Ainsworth. He ’s her attorney.”

“Tell him jest how ’t is, ’Squire.”

“I will.”

“How do you do, Mr. Ainsworth?”

“All right, Mr. Gray. Take a seat.”

"I 've come to see you again in regard to Deacon Wells' business."

"He has. a great deal of trouble in his old age, and it is the result of his own misdeeds."

"Yes, sir. He's in trouble now about his wife's alimony and Harry Jones' suit."

"Does he think he can reduce the alimony?"

"No, sir. He thought the payments were biennial, instead of semi-annual. He cannot meet them, and asks for further time."

"I think there will be no trouble in extending the time. I will see Mrs. Wells about it."

"She will probably be governed by your advice. Will you advise her to extend the time?"

"Yes, sir. I have no desire to persecute the old hypocrite. He has been severely punished already. Now what do you wish to know about Harry Jones' case?"

"I want to compromise it for the very lowest sum that you will take."

"All right. It is generally the best way to dispose of a lawsuit. Mr. Jones will compromise and give a quit-claim deed for four thousand dollars."

"I can get five thousand out of my client, Mr. Ainsworth. Had n't we better settle with Harry for four and divide the other thousand between us?"

"I do n't practice law that way, Mr. Gray. An attorney that will attempt a trick of that kind should be disbarred."

"I mean it for fees, you know. You made my client pay Bessie's fees; why not let him pay Harry's in the same way?"

"That was a very different matter, Mr. Gray. I charged Deacon Wells the regular commission for selling his hemlock bark, and charged Bessie Jones no attorney's fee. It was a legitimate transaction, open and fair. No one was wronged by it, and Bessie Jones was benefited."

"Well; it shall be just as you say. I only wanted fair play between the parties. If a man tries to take the advantage of orphan children, as my client did, I believe in letting him pay for it. You will charge Harry five hundred dollars, I suppose?"

"No, sir. If the case is compromised I shall charge him nothing. Mr. King brought the suit before he went West, and I have had but little work to do."

"It is n't the amount of work an attorney does that should determine his fees. It 's the amount of good he does his client."

"That depends very much on who the attorney is, Esquire. I try to charge according to the work I do."

"An attorney will not get rich if he charges on that principle."

"That will depend very much on the amount of work he does."

"Do n't you do more work in defending a criminal, for the paltry sum of five or ten dollars, than in collecting a thousand-dollar note for which you get fifty?"

"We have a fixed price for collections, excepting cases that are closely litigated; but I sometimes defend a criminal for nothing. It depends on my client's ability to pay. If he is abundantly able to pay fees I charge him the same as I would for equal labor in a civil case. If he is very poor I charge him nothing."

"Do n't you charge a man more when you gain a case than when you lose it?"

"No, sir. I do the best I can for my client, and my services are worth as much when I fail as when I succeed. If a man has a bad case he should not hold his attorney responsible for his failure. If he has a good case, his attorney should not charge an exorbitant fee simply because he succeeds where failure would be the result of carelessness or neglect."

"You have an odd way of charging fees, Mr. Ainsworth."

"It 's an honest way, Esquire."

"Perhaps it is; but it do n't seem to me that it would work well in all cases."

"I find that it works well for me. I do n't dictate to my fellow members of the Bar."

"But you never get a big fee under your rule."

"I get what my services are worth. I have no right to ask more."

"Well; we are getting off the subject. What are your terms of payment for Harry Jones' interest?"

"One thousand dollars down, and three thousand in either annual or biennial payments, with ten per cent. interest, payable annually."

"You may draw up the papers, making the payments biennial."

"All right. I will make out the papers to-morrow."

"You must come up to Mrs. Love's every evening, Robbie. I want to teach you to keep books, write letters, and make yourself generally useful, so that you can go to Nova Scotia next year."

"I 'll come to Mrs. Love's, Miss Jones; but I can't go to Nova Scotia."

"Why not?"

"Mr. Lee won't let me. I 'm bound, you know."

"Yes; you 're bound to go, Robbie. Mr. Wells has made the arrangement with Mr. Lee, and you are to go to him next winter."

"Oh, I 'm so glad. I want to go so much. I know this is some of your work, and I can't repay you for your kindness."

"Yes you can, Robbie."

" How?"

" By trying very hard to learn."

" I can learn without trying very hard, now. I feel like a new boy, already. It will be so nice to be free again."

" Mr. Wells is very kind, Robbie; and if you please him, he will do all in his power to make you happy."

" If I can be useful I shall be very happy, Miss Jones."

" You have much to learn before you can be useful to Mr. Wells, Robbie. He wants you to keep books and attend to his correspóndence. You must learn to write a good hand, use good language, and punctuate correctly."

" I 'll do it, Miss Jones. I 'll study every evening, and you shall see how fast I will learn."

The glad light in the bound boy's eyes was Bessie's reward. What were Robbie's thoughts? " I 'll buy a stone for mother's grave."

" Here is some good news, Bessie. Mr. Ainsworth has compromised with Deacon Wells, and I 'm to have four thousand dollars."

"Your good fortune comes all at once, Harry. James Wells wants you in his law office."

"What can I do in a law office, Bessie?"

"Copy papers, and read law, I suppose. James says you will be useful, and I imagine he knows. He wants some one to take charge of his office while he is in Washington."

"To sit in a chair and tell his clients that he is in Congress. He can put a card on his office door that will do as well."

"He says you will make a good office lawyer, by a little application. He has a fine library which will be at your service, and when he returns your knowledge will be of great value to him."

"And if, in the meantime, a client should propound a question, what could I do?"

"Look wise and — tell him you don't know."

"So I could; and he would believe me, unhesitatingly."

"James wants you, Harry, and I hope you will conclude to go. 'T will be so pleasant for me to have you in Elton this winter."

"It is you he wants, Bessie. I cannot consent to go where I can be only a burden."

"You will not be a burden. If he did not need you he would not ask you to go into his office."

"He is good and noble, Bessie, and he wants me there simply to make it pleasant for you; not for any service that I can render."

"I'll admit that he is good and noble, Harry; and he is also frank and truthful. He is above duplicity, even for a good purpose. If he wanted you to go solely on my account, he would freely tell you so. Wait until you talk with him before you decline his offer. He has made it wholly independent of me, and I firmly believe that you will both be benefited by your labor in his office."

"All right, sister. I'll accept his offer, and I hope you will be equally discreet."

"I have already accepted him, Harry. He is a true man, and I do not fear to place my happiness in his keeping."

"I shall be very proud of my brother-in-law."

"And I shall be very proud of my husband. A year has made a great change in our lives, Harry. A year ago we were struggling to keep the wolf from our door. Now we have enough to support us, and bright prospects for a happy future. Surely, God has been very good to us, and I feel like consecrating my life to His service."

"You have been faithful from your childhood up, dear sister, and you are receiving your reward."

"I have done so little good in the world, Harry."

"You have spent your life in doing good. I tremble when I think of what I would be without you. In our dark days your faith and gentle teaching saved me. Even now I should be lost in doubt but for your guidance."

"You cannot doubt that God is good."

"I do not doubt that He is good to you and to me, Bessie, but there are so many deserving ones that He forgets."

"He does not forget them, Harry."

"He permits them to suffer so much."

"It is for some wise purpose. Everything in nature testifies to His goodness. This we cannot doubt. While there is much that we cannot comprehend, we can understand His love and His mercy; His munificence and His care."

"I know it, Bessie. When you are near me I never doubt; but when you are absent, God seems a great way off."

"That is because you do not try to get near Him, Harry."

"I will try to live nearer to Him in the future, sister."

"You will find that He is very near you, when you earnestly invoke His presence."

"You must go with me to Washington, mother. I shall be very lonely without you, and it will do you good to see a little of the world."

"Do n't urge me to go, James."

"Why not?"

"I should feel sadly out of place. I want to stay here and take care of the house."

"I shall shut the house up, mother."

"What will you do with your horses and cow?"

"Board them out."

"Then there's the cat and the birds. You

have quite a family, James, and you had better let me stay and take care of them."

"They shall be provided for, mother. I can't get along without you. If you are not happy there you can return and open the house; but you need a change. You look weary, and I know you will be benefited by a visit to Washington."

"I cannot enjoy Washington society, James. I prefer this quiet life."

"There are real folks in Washington, mother. You need not mingle with the gay and thoughtless. Society is much as it is in other cities. We have the good and the bad; the real and the seeming. You can choose your associates."

"The fact that I am a divorced wife is an ever present sorrow, my dear boy. I do not want any associates. I do not want to mingle with the world. I feel the disgrace, and cannot forget it."

"You are not disgraced. You are honored and loved by all who know you, mother."

"I am 'honored and loved' by a dutiful son; and I know I am selfish in my sorrow. You have done so much to make me happy, James, that I sometimes feel guilty because I cannot fully enjoy all that your kind care and thoughtful attention provide; but the old, tired feeling comes unbidden, and I cannot shake it off. Leave me here, and let me rest until you return."

"No, mother; you must go with me. There is a place in the great world for you. Your work is not done."

It is seldom that a strong man's will is successfully opposed by woman. Patience Wells went to Washington. James secured rooms in a private boarding house, with a pleasant family, introduced his mother to a few of his tried friends, took her through the public buildings, accompanied her to church, and spent all his leisure hours in her cosy sitting room. He was chairman of an important committee, and was emphatically a "working member," yet he devoted much time to his mother, and did everything in his power to make her visit to the Capital City profitable and pleasant. She was a good conversationist, and her society was sought by a circle of admiring friends. While she was comparatively ignorant of the ways of the world, her rare good sense and ready tact enabled her to avoid mistakes. She was active in public and private charities, active in the church, and foremost in all good works. James was liberal, and she was his almoner. He managed to bring her in contact with those whom he knew would be congenial, hoping by that means to cause her to forget the past and live only in the present. His father's name was never mentioned, and he imagined that the wounds were healing. He did not dream that his mother was making a great sacrifice to please him.

"My letter was from Bessie, James."

"I supposed so, mother. The superscription had a familiar look."

"She says Robbie Bently is getting along finely with his studies. He is already proficient in book-keeping, and she sent a specimen of his penmanship that is very creditable."

"I am glad he is making rapid progress. It is no more than I expected. Bessie is very anxious for his success, and she will strive to qualify him for his work."

"Bessie is a dear, good girl, James."

" We agree on that point, mother. I heartily indorse your sentiments, and shall vote in the affirmative."

" Come, my boy; you are not in the House."

" I am not in the street, mother."

" You might as well be in the street, for I can't make you talk seriously about Bessie Jones."

" That 's because I do n't feel ' serious ' when I think of her."

" It is time for you to think seriously of marrying her, my son."

" I 'm ready, mother. The ceremony may be performed whenever it suits you and Bessie."

" I am not to be consulted in the matter."

" Then you do n't believe in match-making? "

" No, I do not. Two can wind yarn successfully, but when the third party interferes the skein is tangled, and a lifetime will prove too short to unravel it. I 've seen too many unhappy marriages grow out of a mother's interference."

" But you would not have me marry without your consent, mother?"

" Your wish shall be my law, James. Children should judge for themselves in a matter so important."

"Yet it is better to have the consent of parents?"

"Yes. If parents and children act wisely; but it is often the case that children yield blindly to the wishes of parents, and find, too late, that they have committed a fatal error. Marriage without love is a crime, and the penalty is more than death. A great many unfortunate marriages result from the unwise dictation of parents."

"That is true, mother, and I have taken the precaution to first arrange matters and then ask your consent."

"You have acted wisely, my son. When are you to be married?"

"I shall let you and Bessie determine that matter."

"Let Bessie fix the time, James. She is the party most deeply interested."

"Am not I as deeply interested, mother?"

"No."

"Why not?"

"Simply because you are a man. A woman

resigns everything to the keeping of her husband when she marries. A man does not so completely give himself up to his wife. He has a world outside of his home; but home is all the world to the wife."

" I can't see it in that light, mother."

" I see it from a woman's standpoint, James."

" It shall not be so in my case, mother. My home shall be as much my world as Bessie's."

" You will be very happy together. She is a true woman, and I 'm glad you have chosen her. You are worthy of all the love she can bestow."

" With your blessing our home shall be bright and happy, dear mother."

" God will bless your home, my boy."

" I could not ask His blessing if yours were withheld, mother."

" It is His province to bless you; mine to live in a borrowed light."

" Good morning, Mrs. Wells. I 'm on my way to Mrs. Gregg's, and I have called for you to go with me. We want the assistance of all the philanthropic women in the city."

19

"I am not a philanthropist, Mrs. Derby; but you can tell me the object of your meeting."

"We want to establish a home for friendless women."

"Is there not an institution of that kind already established?"

"Yes; but it is n't well managed. There are but few inmates, and no effort is made to increase the number. The city is full of fallen women, and we propose to go among them, convince them that we are really interested in their welfare, and save as many as possible."

"Would it not be better to co-operate with the managers of the present institution than to establish another?"

"We will talk that over at Mrs. Gregg's. The impression prevails that there is too much silk and satin about the present institution. It is managed by fashionable women, whose hearts are not in the work. They flatter the men who are responsible for the fall of some of the inmates, and draw their costly robes about them when they meet a fallen sister, as though the touch would contaminate them. We want earnest workers, Mrs. Wells. We want women."

" 'T is my conviction that the way to work effectually is to reform the men; but I will go with you."

" We can't reform the men without the co-operation of fashionable women. They do not hold a man responsible for his sins. Even mothers fail to reprove their sons. So long as this state of affairs exists, we can't reform the men."

" And so long as men are base, we can't reform the women, Mrs. Derby."

" I know it is a hard task, especially in this city; but we can do some good. I do n't believe in folding our hands and doing nothing, because we can't do it all, Mrs. Wells."

" Neither do I. We will go to work and do what we can. Even if one be reclaimed, we shall be compensated."

Patience Wells worked with a will in the new field that had been opened to her. She was singularly successful in winning the erring ones, and for the first time in many years she forgot the past and lived for others. She found many who gladly left the haunts of vice and entered upon a new life with a determination to reform.

Most of these were reclaimed, and have outlived their sin. A small number — too weak to resist temptation — went back to the old life, and are suffering the penalty of their transgression. Patience was untiring in her efforts to save them, and often induced them to enter the "home" a second time. In all cases — where the sin was not inherent — she worked hopefully, determined to do her whole duty and leave the result with Him who notes the falling of a sparrow. She was not surprised to find, among the erring, many discarded wives who had "married for a home." To these her heart went out in sympathy, for she knew how sorely they were tempted. She knew that the libertine instinctively sought an unloved wife. When will the mothers in our land learn to give their daughters a practical education, and place them beyond the necessity of marrying for a home? Until this lesson is learned there will be no lack of inmates in the homes for friendless women.

———

"Good mornin', sir. Your name's George Wells, I b'leve?"

"Yes, sir."

"Well, my name's Jack Blunt. You used to know me when I's a little boy. I've been a purty hard ticket for a good many years, but if you'll give me somethin' to do I'll reform and be a man agin."

"What can you do, Jack?"

"I'm willin' to turn my hand to anything, sir. I can load plaster, if you've nothin' else for me to do."

"I have a dozen idle men under pay now, Jack."

"You do n't pay 'em when they do n't work, do you?"

"Yes, sir. They are willing to work, and I can't let them starve."

"You're the kind of a boss for me. I'll take a wheelbarrer at a shillin' a day, ruther than miss."

"I do n't want you to work for a shilling a day. I do n't need you at any price, Jack; but if you really desire to reform I'll give you work."

"That's what's the matter of me. I'm goin' to reform. Nelly, that's my darter, is gittin' well, and I'm goin' to git a little home for her and be a man agin, if you and God will let me."

"That is an irreverent speech, Jack."

"What kind of a speech, Mr. Wells?"

"Irreverent; disrespectful. You should not speak of God in that manner. He will let you reform and will help you if you will ask Him."

"You must excuse me, Mr. Wells. I hain't got no religion and I'm sorry for it. I wan't raised that way; but I'll try to be better if you'll give me a fair chance."

"I'll give you work, Jack, and you must ask God to make you better."

"Won't He say ' It's nobody but Jack Blunt,' if I ask Him?"

"No. Jack Blunt is as dear to Him as any of His creatures."

"But He knows I used to smuggle rum."

"He is merciful and will forgive you if you ask Him in the right spirit."

"And will He forgive me for apprisin' the Jones place too low?"

"Yes, sir."

"And cheatin' at ten cent ante?"

"Yes, sir."

"And swindlin' Uncle Henry out o' these boots?"

"No, sir. You can pay for the boots. You must not ask God to forgive you for a wrong that you can right."

"All right. I 'll pay for these boots out o' the fust money I git."

"I 'll advance you the money to pay for them if you wish it."

"No, sir. Let him wait till I earn it. He told me when I got 'em that I 'd never pay for 'em, and I b'leved him. He 'll be pleasantly disappinted when he gits a letter from Jack Blunt inclosin' five dollars for these boots."

" Do you owe any other little bills, Jack?"

" No, sir. Nothin' but some away back, and I guess God 'll have no trouble forgittin' them, 'cause I 've almost forgot 'em myself."

" You must pay them up and commence right."

"Jest as you say, Mr. Wells."

" You will feel better if you begin right, Jack. Honesty pays large dividends."

" Then I want to git into it. Do you think God 'll forgive me for swearin' like a pirate?"

"Yes.   He will forgive you if you ask him in the right spirit, and resolve to swear no more."

"He's got a big contract, Mr. Wells; but I'll take your word for it and stop swearin'."

"You must take His word, Jack.   Have you a Bible?"

"No, sir.   Nelly had one, but I found a famly in Elton that had n't got none, and I thought it was my duty to give it to 'em.   I hain't had none sense; but I'll git one as soon as I pay for these boots."

"Here's one that you may have, Jack."

"Do you give away Bibles?"

"Sometimes."

"I guess the plaster bizness must be good if you can 'ford to pay men for doin' nothin' and give away Bibles to boot."

"I do n't usually pay men for doing nothing. These are dull times, Jack, and I have no work for some of my men. They must live, you know."

"Do you take it out o' their wages when they go to work agin?"

"No, sir."

"Well, you air an odd chicken.   I 've heered

Parson Green talk about practising Christians, but you 're the fust one I ever met, onless it were the Parson hisself."

"Then you 've heard Parson Green preach?"

"Yes, sir. I used to go to please Nelly, afore she went crazy. I hain't went to no good places sense Nelly went crazy. Somehow I hain't had no appertite for good things. I guess the devil's been foolin' 'round me."

"You say Nellie is getting better?"

"Yes, sir. Here's the letter that says she's almost well, and 't will make a man of Jack Blunt yit, if he is a poor coot."

"I hope so."

"And you shan't be disappinted, Mr. Wells. I 've got somethin' to live for now. I got sort o' reckless after Nelly was took away, and I wan't an angel afore; but you 'll find me here every time from this on, and if ever I swear or tell a lie, may the good Lord forgit it alongst the balance of 'em."

"I am glad that you are going to try to reform, Jack."

"Try? I 'm goin' to make it. You 're the fust Christian, exceptin' Parson Green, that ever tried to make me better. Christians is allers so fur off that we poor devils can't git to 'em. I did n't mind the Parson 'cause I thought 't was his reg'lar bizness, but your bizness is shippin' land plaster and I know you 're in dead earnest when you ketch a feller by the nap o' the neck and try to pull him into Heaven."

" That 's a queer way to get a man to Heaven, Jack. You must remember that God, alone, can open the door to His kingdom."

" He might open the door till the cows come home and we poor devils would never find it without some good, geniwine Christian to show us the way; and I 'm much obliged to you for showin' me the way, Mr. Wells."

" I have not shown you the way, Jack. Read that book carefully, ask God to give you light, and you will find the way."

"Shall I come to you when I git stuck?"

" No."

" Where shall I go?"

" Go to God."

" All right, Mr. Wells; I 'll go, but I do n't b'leve He 's knowd me sense I wore trowsers."

" Seek Him in a proper spirit, Jack, and you

will find Him. Go to Him to-night, and come to work in the morning."

" Thank you, sir. I 'll go, and come."

Jack Blunt was sincere in his desire to go to God. The kindness of Mr. Wells warmed his heart and brought forth the little good that was in it. There are many Jack Blunts in the world, but they do not find a George Wells to pull them through when they " get stuck " in the slough of doubt.

CHAPTER XIII.

HEELING AND TOEING.

CAN you tap 'em right on the spot, Uncle Henry?"

"No, Bob; you 'll have to take them off your feet."

"I mean, can you tap them now?"

"Why did n't you say so?"

"Well, most anybody but you would understood me."

"What 's your great hurry, Bob?"

"I 'm goin' to Spring River lake after trout in the mornin', and I want to wear 'em."

"The trout?"

"No; the boots. Me and Sam White is goin' to take a cold bite and then start afore breakfast."

"You 'll get a ' cold bite ' before you get back, if this weather holds."

"So he will, Uncle Henry. He 'll find that

the wind and frost and everything but the trout
will bite."

"Steve Garret ketched a nine pound trout out
o' there last week, and I 'm as good a fisherman
as he is."

" Did you see that trout?"

"No; but I heered about it."

" That 's the trouble.   You are always hearing
about big trout, but no one sees them.   I 've
been here sixty years, and have fished in all the
lakes between the Penobscot and St. Croix, but
I never saw one of the regular brook trout spe-
cies that measured over twenty-three inches, or
weighed over five pounds.   I do n't believe
there's a nine pound speckled trout in the State
of Maine."

" There 's the difference 'twixt us.   I believe
Washington county is full of 'em."

" The oldest inhabitant never saw them, and
the latest arrival won't live long enough to put
his two eyes on them."

" Wait 'till I git back, Uncle Henry.   I 'll
show you a golly-buster."

"The ice is two feet thick, Bob, and you 'll
freeze before you can cut a hole through it."

"Do n't fret about my freezin'. I ain't so dredful tender."

"If he can only protect his head he 'll get through all right, Uncle Henry."

"But there 's the rub, Charles."

"And it 'll keep him rubbin' all the time to save them ears o' his."

"Give us a rest, Mountain Jack. You ain't runnin' this show."

"If I was I 'd put the long eared critters on the other side of the stove, and give the visiters a chance to warm."

"What are you going to bait with, Bob?"

"Clams."

"Shelled?"

"Of course. Who ever heered of a trout bitin' a clam that was n't shelled?"

"Who ever heard of a trout biting a shelled clam?"

"I have. Steve Garret ketched his big trout with a shelled clam, and I 'm goin' to git one jest like it for the mistress. She ain't very well, and she 's 'mazin' fond of 'em."

"Of clams?"

"No, trout."

"Why did n't you say so?"

"I did, but you could n't understand. Seems to me you 're all dredful dull this evenin'."

"We 're too sharp to believe your big trout story."

"Seein's believin', and I 'll show you when I git back."

"I hope you 'll get a trout for the teacher, Bob; but I 'll make you a pair of boots for every pound he weighs over five."

"Then you need n't be so dredful pertickeler about mendin' them old ones. I 'll have two or three new pair comin' when I git back."

"I guess I 'll peg these soles on pretty stout. You 'll have to wear them awhile."

"Did you say Miss Jones is n't very well, Bob?"

"That 's jest what I said. You seem to understand that well enough; but you need n't worry about her. Jim Wells will take her in tow when he gits back from Congress."

"What's the matter with her?"

"She 's been working nights to git Ragged Bob ready to go to Novy Skoshy."

"How is he getting along?"

"Fust rate. He can pass any sentence in the book, and he writes as purty as the teacher, already, and he do n't have to go 'til next fall."

"I 'm glad Robbie is going. He 's a bright boy and he deserves a good chance."

"They say old Wells is goin' to give him a big send off when he gits him there."

"I hope he will. The poor fellow has had a hard time at Mr. Lee's."

"Bound boys allers has a hard time, do n't they, Charley?"

"Not always. Johnny Bell is happy."

"Yes, but Johnny is bound to a Christian."

"Is n't Robbie Bently bound to a Christian?"

"Well, I do n't know. Mr. Lee ain't Christian enough to hurt him any; but Mr. Noel is an every day Christian. He 's allers good; while Mr. Lee is good by spells. Mr. Noel is one of Parson Green's Christians, and they 're a mighty sight better than common ones."

"Mr. Lee always conducts himself like a Christian. He seems to me a very devout man."

"What 's devout?"

"Pious."

" *A hoss-trade between two Christians aint allers a Christian hoss-trade* "—PAGE 306.

"That's because you do n't know him. He's like lots of other Christians; all right 'til you git clost to him. There's a devil in him bigger'n a hedge-hog. He'd do anything for money, and them kind o' Christians won't do to make fast to; they pull out too easy."

"I know he is prudent, but I do n't believe he'd do anything wrong to get money."

"You do n't, hey? Look at that hoss he sold Elder Steele. He ain't wuth fifty dollars, and he sold him for a hundred and seventy-five."

"But he gave fifty dollars of the amount for preaching."

"That was done jest to sell the hoss. He never give more 'n five dollars a year, afore. That's one of Lee's Yankee tricks."

"Was n't the Elder satisfied with his bargain?"

"Satisfied! He tried to sell him back the next week for seventy-five dollars, and Lee told him he had all the hosses he could winter. He's a reg'lar plug, and ain't wuth nothin' to pull."

"Why did n't he bring the matter before the church?"

20

"A hoss trade's a hoss trade, in this country, and the church could n't make nothin' out of it."

"But swindling is swindling, in this country, and the church could make something out of that."

"Lee did n't warrant the hoss to pull. He jest told the Elder he had a gentle hoss and he asked a hundred and seventy-five dollars for him, but seein' 't was him he 'd let him go for a hundred and twenty-five cash, and give fifty for preachin'. That's the way they fixed it."

"Is the horse gentle?"

"He 's so gentle he won't start if you build a fire under him."

"But he can't compel the Elder to keep him."

"No. The Elder can trade him off to somebody else, if he wants to, but he can't git him back on Lee. A hoss trade between two Christians ain't allers a Christian hoss trade."

"I 'll bait a nine-pence that Lee could n't git to windward of Parson Green in a hoss trade."

"No; 'cause he 's a good judge of a hoss."

"Yes; and he 's a good judge of men, too."

"He 's a reg'lar brick."

"He 's a genuine Christian."

"So he is, Uncle Henry; but he knows somethin' besides what's in the Bible."

"Yes; he knows all about the Bible, and some things outside of it. He knows enough about the world to make him a useful preacher."

"Dad says he's a better lawyer than 'Squire Gray."

"'Squire Gray ain't a lawyer any more. Mr. Ainsworth had him turned out."

"I've heered of a church that was so bad that they could n't turn a man out 'cause there was no place to turn him to, but I'd like to know where they'd turn a lawyer."

"He has been disbarred, Sam."

"What's that?"

"Barred out."

"He cannot practice before the courts. He was charged with unprofessional conduct, and the charge was sustained."

"What did he do?"

"He tried to swindle Deacon Wells out of a thousand dollars."

"It do n't seem to me there was anything unprofeshunal about that."

"The members of the Bar looked at it in a different light, Sam."

" Is lawyers gittin' onest? "

" Were they not always honest? "

" Dad says not. When mam told him I 'd make a fust rate lawyer, he said I was too onest for a lawyer and would do better sawin' wood."

" That ain't what you 's born for, Sam."

" What was I born for, Jack? "

" Settin' for picters in a country where they raise corn."

" You 're too cute to live in Maine, Mountain Jack. You orter go to Novy Skoshy alongst Jack Blunt."

. "The mistress got a letter from Jim Wells' uncle, to-day, and he says Jack Blunt has reformed and is a good Christian."

" Well, I declare! That 's 'mazin' surprisin', as Aunty Marsh says."

" Not very surprising, Uncle Henry. Jack is a kind hearted man, and there 's always a chance for such a man to repent."

" Yes; he has some good streaks, but they are like streaks of fat in a potato-fed pig — rather seldom."

"If he will serve the Lord as well as he has served the devil, he will make a very good Christian."

"He can't do that."

"Why not?"

"He is fifty years old, and his working days are over."

"Can't the Lord renew his strength?"

"The Lord does n't work that way, Charley. If a man spends his best days in working for the devil, he can't ask the Lord to give him a new lease of life, even to devote to His service."

"Do you s'pose Jack Blunt will stick?"

"Why not?"

"Oh, he 's a rattler, and them church meetin's will be too dull for him."

"Parson Green's church meetings are not dull."

"But there ain't many Parson Greens. Novy Skoshy ain't settled with 'em."

"There ain't enough Parson Greens in the world, I 'll admit, Sam; but maybe Jack will run afoul of one down there."

"I hope he will, for I 'd like to see Jack stick."

"Then why do n't you follow his example, Sam?"

"There 's lots of time.   I 'm only eighteen."

"That 's the devil's argument.   God says: 'They that seek me early shall find me.' There 's danger in delay."

"But I want to have a good time, Uncle Henry, and I can't do it if I jine church."

"That 's another one of the devil's arguments. You can enjoy yourself in serving the Lord.   It is the only real pleasure I ever had in this world, and the only joy that I hope for in the next."

"I want to take most of mine in the next."

"You can't spend your days in sinning and fully enjoy the next, even if you do repent at the eleventh hour."

"What do you know about religion, Charley?"

"Not much, I 'll admit; but it do n't look reasonable that Jack Blunt should enjoy so much of Heaven as Parson Green "

"Heaven is Heaven, Charley, and if a man is fortunate enough to get there he 'll enjoy it.   I do n't believe in these new fangled ideas about progression and degrees of happiness.   When a man's happy, he's happy. That's plain enough, is n't it?"

" Yes, sir."

" Well, when a man's cup of happiness is full, what's the use of running it over? Heaven will fill everybody's cup, and the fool will be as happy as the wise man there. There's nothing in the Bible about one man enjoying more than another in Heaven."

" This is God's earth, Uncle Henry, and why should one man enjoy more than another here?"

" There is no comparison between earth and Heaven, Charley. The fool enjoys more than the wise man, here. If his enjoyment depended on his knowledge, this would not be. Circumstances make us happy or unhappy here. It will not be so in Heaven."

" I'm not willing to admit that the fool enjoys more than the wise man here."

" Observation will teach you that, Charley."

" My observation has not taught me that the ignorant are happier than the wise."

" Then you are not a careful observer. Show me a happier man than Enoch West, and he do n't know enough to warm his feet when they 're cold."

"Jim Wells is as happy as he."

"Jim Wells is an exception among wise men, and still I do n't believe he 's as happy as Enoch."

"He is always cheerful."

"You do n't see him 'always,' Charley. Perhaps he keeps his 'skeleton in the closet.' There 's many a sad heart veiled by a cheerful face."

CHAPTER XIV.

AT HOME.

SAY four weeks, Bessie. Two months seems a long time to wait."

"I can't get ready in four weeks, James."

"Why not?"

"There are so many little things to do."

"Leave them undone until after our marriage, Bessie."

"There are some things that must be done before. I can't possibly get ready in four weeks, but will compromise with you and say six weeks from to-day."

"All right. As we may have to compromise our differences after marriage, perhaps it will be well to commence before."

"We will have no differences after marriage, James."

"I hope not; but we are human."

"Aye; and we realize it. That will prevent discord. I think our married life will be singularly happy. We know each other so well."

"Yes, Bessie; you know all my weak points, and will take the step with your eyes open."

"I do not hesitate to risk my happiness in your hands. I have not discovered the weak points you speak of."

"Love is blind, you know."

"My love is not blind, James. If there were weak points in your character I could see them."

"I am painfully conscious of their existence, Bessie."

"As I have looked for them in vain, I will take your word and look no further. I shall never discover them."

"You cannot fail to see, and I hope you will correct them."

"I laid aside the rod when my school closed."

"You will still be a teacher, Bessie."

"Then we will have to vary the rule. I shall recite to my pupil."

"You must help me brush up my Greek and Latin."

"I am better qualified to brush your coat."

"You are incorrigible."

"Then you will not attempt to correct me?"

"No. I shall turn you over to mother."

"You will leave me in excellent hands. I love your mother."

"So do I. We agree on that point."

"Your mother has been very kind to me, and I am so glad she will live with us."

"With mother, Harry, and an occasional visit from Uncle George, we shall be very happy, Bessie."

"God is good."

"What kind of a wedding do you want, Bessie?"

"You must consult James on that point, mother."

"I like to have you call me 'mother,' my dear child."

"I am so grateful for the privilege. My dead mother comes to me in my dreams, and thus I keep her image in my memory. I was so young when she died that I feared I should not know her in another world."

"My experience is not unlike yours, my dear child. My mother died when I was three years old, and in my orphanage I felt the need of her protecting care. We met in dreamland, and took sweet counsel together in that unreal world. To me it was more than seeming. Like you, I taught school several years, and when my burden seemed more than I could bear, her presence gave me strength and courage. There is nothing so dear to the orphan's heart as the memory of mother."

" 'T will be so nice to have a living, breathing mother; one to whom I can come for counsel and advice; one whom I can touch, obey, and kiss. I shall love you very much, dear mother."

"Not more than I shall love you, my child. But about the wedding? I ask James, and he refers me to you. I ask you, and you tell me to consult James. Speak out, Bessie, and tell me whether you want a public or a private wedding."

"I prefer a very quiet wedding, mother."

"So does James. Now that point is settled. Shall the ceremony be performed here?"

"As you like. I have no foolish scruples

about the propriety, mother; but would prefer to go quietly to the parsonage and have the ceremony performed in presence of a few dear friends. I presume James wants Parson Green to officiate?"

"Yes, dear. If he is acceptable to you."

"He is my choice, mother."

"It shall be as you suggest. James has expressed a wish to be married at the parsonage."

"Then that question is settled."

"Yes. Shall he write to his Uncle George?"

"By all means. Our happiness would not be complete without him."

"I 'll write to George myself. It may be too late when James returns. He asked me to see you and 'arrange things.' His unexpected call to Washington gave him no time to attend to the details, but we will do very well without him."

"Yes, mother; we can make the necessary arrangements in his absence."

"He 'll be here in time for the ceremony."

"If not, we can tell our friends it will be 'postponed on account of the weather.'"

"Would n't 'for want of a bridegroom' be better?"

"Won't the weather be 'stormy' if the bride-groom does n't come at the appointed time?"

"No, dearie. The little cloud would be dissipated when he did come. There will be no storms in your life, either before or after marriage."

"I believe you, dear mother. I feel that my married life will be all sunshine."

James returned a few hours before the time appointed for the ceremony. Uncle George was present, and of the small but merry party assembled at Parson Green's, none, save the bride and groom, were happier than he. "What, therefore, God hath joined together let not man put asunder." No lingering doubt disturbed Parson Green. Surely, God had joined James Wells and Bessie Jones.

"And now, Bessie, I want to know how my young book-keeper is getting along. Is he ready to go back with me?"

"He is qualified, Uncle George, and if Mr. Lee will consent you can take him with you, but we do n't intend to let you go at present. You are to visit Niagara and the Hudson with us."

"And spoil your wedding tour?"

"By no means. Your presence will add to our happiness."

"I think I shall take Robbie and return. I did n't make arrangements for a protracted visit. If I can leave my business with Robbie I shall see you next winter — perhaps go to Washington with you."

"I am not an active member of Congress, and shall probably remain at home during the session; but it will be very pleasant for mother and me to have you with us while James is away."

"And I flatter myself that it will be pleasant for James to have me visit him in Washington, Mrs. Wells."

"So it will; but we are in the majority, and he must yield."

"He may prove a very stubborn minority, Bessie."

"No, Uncle; he will yield gracefully when he is voted down."

"Perhaps your mother will vote with him."

"Here she is. Ask her."

"Are you going to Washington, next winter, Patience?"

"That will be as James says. I should like to go."

"There, Bessie. We will all go to Congress."

"Then I shall have to yield. That's the way it goes. The 'lords of creation' have their own way when they really want it."

"Yes; and poor, down-trodden women must submit, be dragged out into the world, wear silk dresses, and eat confectionery."

"That is not the end of their submission, Uncle George."

"No. They must entertain the men of state, and captivate sages and philosophers by their bewitching airs and bright glances."

"That is sarcasm, Uncle George, and it needs no label."

"It will be true in your case, Bessie."

"If I can hold captive one of the wise men of the nation, and retain his uncle's esteem, my ambition will be fully satisfied."

"That is already assured; and now, like a veritable queen, you must increase the number of your subjects."

"I prefer a small kingdom and loyal subjects. My heart is too small to divide into parcels."

"The human heart is an enigma, Bessie. It is increased by division."

"You may be right, but I have no desire to try the experiment."

"It is not an experiment. It is an established fact."

"I shall not divide mine in Washington, Uncle George."

"But I shall take a little piece of it to Nova Scotia, my dear niece."

"I hope you will take more than a 'little piece of it,' dear Uncle; but you must bring it back to Maine in the early autumn."

"So I will, if my life be spared."

———

"Good morning, Mr. Lee. I've come to see if you'll let Robbie go home with me."

"I can't let him go 'til next winter."

"Why not?"

"Because that is the contract, and I want him to get my winter's wood."

"What will it cost to cut your wood?"

"About thirty dollars."

"Here are your thirty dollars. Tell Robbie

to pack his trunk. I shall start next Monday morning.”

“ He has n't any trunk.”

“ How will he take his clothes? ”

“ On his back, all but an extra shirt and pair of socks.”

“ You will please give him this note, and tell him to buy a traveling bag.”

“ I 've got an old one that I can sell him cheap. I 'll hunt it up.”

“ All right. I 'll get him some clothes at St. John.”

“ I 'd have got them, Mr. Wells, but this is a very poor place to buy clothes.”

“ It seems so.”

Early on Monday morning Robbie called to say good bye to Bessie Wells.

“ Be a good boy, Robbie; attend faithfully to your business, and, above all things, be particular in choosing your associates.”

“ I will try to do as you wish, Mrs. Wells. I owe you so much. You have been very kind to me, and, excepting Mr. Wells, you are my only friend.”

“ You forget your best friend, Robbie.”

"I should not have known Him if you had not taught me."

"When you are tired and homesick, Robbie, you must go to Him for comfort."

"I shall not be homesick if you will write to me. I have no one else in Elton to care for."

"I will write to you often. Good bye."

"Good bye, Mrs. Wells. God will bless you for your kindness to me."

"Remember, always, Robbie, that God is good."

"I will remember."

Robbie Bently kept his word. He was ever mindful of his employer's interest, and very soon learned the routine of business. He knew that Mr. Wells would spend the winter with his nephew, and he resolved to render a good account of his stewardship when his employer returned.

"I shall be gone four months, Robbie. Your position is a responsible one, and you will have no friend to advise you. Do the best you can, and remember, always, to do right, regardless of consequences."

"I will try to do as you wish, Mr. Wells."

"All right, my boy. I think you will have no trouble in managing the business."

Mr. Wells called his employes together, told them Robbie was authorized to transact his business during his absence, and requested respectful obedience. Robbie was popular with the men, and was successful in managing them. During Mr. Wells absence the business rapidly increased. The men, remembering his kindness, cheerfully worked over-time, and Robbie was not compelled to employ additional help.

"Robbie, you'll have to keep your eye on Bill Jenkins."

"Why, Jack?"

"He's tryin' to git some of the men to strike for higher wages. I don't like to 'blow,' but Mr. Wells has been good to you and me, and one good turn deserves another. You'd better turn Bill off."

"He is an old hand, is n't he?"

"About forty, I guess."

"I mean, he has been in the employ of Mr. Wells for some time."

"Oh, yes. He'd a starved to death last winter if the boss had n't fed him."

"Are any others discontented?"

"No, sir. They 're true as steel."

"Has Bill talked to many of the men?"

"He's talked to me and Charley Hay, and Bob Childs, and Ben Dillingham. I do n't know how many more. We told him to save his breath 'til times got dull agin, and then use it in askin' the boss for bread and meat for his children."

"What reply did he make?"

"He said he did n't want to work under a boy what had n't no beard on his face. I 'd let him go quicker 'n shootin', Robbie."

"How many children has he?"

"Four or five."

"I 'll talk to him, Jack."

"Talk sassy to him, Robbie. I 've been a purty good Christian for a year, but I 'll git a furlough long enough to lick him for you, if you want me to."

"What do you want to whip him for?"

"For sayin' you hain't got no beard."

"That is the truth, Jack. I hope you would n't whip a man for telling the truth."

"'T ain't his place to tell it. You do n't seem

like a boy no more, Robbie; and if he 'd kep his
clack shet the men would n't a knowed you had
no hair on your face."

"I do n't care what Bill says about me, Jack.
If he will work for his employer's interest I 'll
not discharge him."

"Well, Robbie, I s'pose you 're right, but you
can stan' more 'n me."

"I will see Bill, to-morrow. He must stop
talking such stuff to the men."

Robbie "talked to" Bill Jenkins the next day.
He reminded him of Mr. Wells' kindness during
the dark days of the previous winter, and soon
brought the tears to the man's eyes.

"I s'pose I 'll git my walkin' papers, Mr.
Bently?"

"No; I do n't want to discharge you, William.
I want you to work for the interest of the man
who has befriended you, and not try to make
others discontented."

"I s'pose you 'll report me to the boss when
he comes home?"

"If you do your duty from this time until his
return, there will be nothing to report."

"Here's my hand, young man. I'll remember this lesson."

After that "talk," no man worked more faithfully for Mr. Wells than Bill Jenkins. If all employers were as wise and humane as George Wells there would be few "strikes" and far less suffering among the laboring classes. Until employers know more of their men than can be gleaned by a glance at the pay roll, there will be no solution of the vexed "labor question."

George Wells spent a pleasant winter in Washington with James, Bessie and Patience. He was proud of his nephew, whom the best men in the nation delighted to honor, and — strange as it may appear — he was pleased with Washington society. Early in the spring he returned to Windsor to "give Robbie a rest."

"Well, my boy, how did you get along with that last cargo?"

"All right, Mr. Wells. When I wrote you, I thought you would have to pay demurrage, but the men worked so faithfully that the vessel was not detained."

"They are good men, Robbie, and are always ready to do their whole duty."

"Yes, sir. They have worked well. I have paid all bills, and here is a statement of the business transacted during your absence. I have not included the plaster on hand, but I think there is fully as much as when you left."

"There is more, Robbie. I looked at it as I came in. Thirty-one hundred dollars net profits! Why, my boy, you do better when I am gone than when I am here to bother you."

"No, sir. I miss you very much. But business was better after you left, and prices were higher."

"But you have handled an unusual quantity of plaster without increasing the number of men."

"I had them work over-time. I thought it would be better than to employ more men."

"You acted wisely, Robbie. Hereafter you may conduct. the business in the name of Wells & Bently."

"But you don't intend to give me an interest in the business, Mr. Wells?"

"No; I don't intend to give it to you. You have earned it, my boy, and I shall not withhold it."

"This is too much, Mr. Wells. I cannot repay you."

"You'd better go and tell the men they can have a holiday, Robbie."

With tears of gratitude the orphan boy obeyed. He could not utter his thanks. He would place a stone at the grave of his mother and sisters.

———

"I'll have to let the Jones place go, Elijah. I can't meet them payments and keep it."

"It's the best payin' property you've got, father."

"I know it; but it must be sold."

"We're gittin' purty near the poor house, father."

"So we air."

"If you hadn't been a fool, we'd be forehanded this blessed minit."

"You're a fine speciment to call your father a fool."

"That's jest what you air, dad. If you'd staid in prison we'd a been all right."

"And you think I hain't got no more sprawl

than to stay in prison to save money for you, do you? I 've told you afore that you can't play your father for a nateral fool."

"If you 'd staid in prison you would n't had no forty thousand dollars divorce money to pay, and 'Squire Gray would n't a got that thirty thousand dollars' wuth of property for gittin' you out."

"If you had n't writ that deed we would n't been in prison."

"'T was your signin' it that sent us."

"If you 'd a been half as smart as Jim you could a marrid Bessie Jones, and we would n't had no trouble."

"Marryin' a gal agin her will is hard bizness in this country, dad."

"Well, there 'll be enough left to keep me, and you can dig clams for a livin', for all I care."

"That 's as good as smugglin' rum."

"Go right off to bed, Elijah."

———

Uncle Henry is still working hemlock tan and listening to the gossips. His little shop is nightly filled with good, bad, and indifferent

Eltonians. He has tried in vain to reform the bad. Philip, the philosopher, calls in when he thinks the severe weather will keep the scandal-mongers at home. He and Uncle Henry are still of the opinion that "Parson Green is the best Christian in Maine."

Elder Steele has gone West. He found that Elton was not like an omnibus.

Widow Love is still jolly. She scatters a great deal of sunshine, and is especially kind to the fatherless. When the night is very cold, the Glenville and Berwick stage stops before her door, and the passengers wonder "what's up." In two minutes the driver is again in his seat, warmed and cheered by the cup of hot coffee he has "jest put down."

Nelly Blunt is living with her father, in the little home he has provided. She is not insane, but there is no joy in her heart, and she is sadly awaiting the summons that is delayed only when the weary soul would gladly obey.

James Wells is still in Congress, serving his third term. He stoutly maintains that he is not a politician; but he is deeply interested in the moves on the political checker-board. He stands at the head of his profession, and is beloved by all who know him.

Harry Jones is already a "good office lawyer," and the business of Wells & Jones is lucrative and satisfactory.

Ben Love and Zach Brown have grown up and gone West. They are honest and true, and if they can manage to keep out of Congress they will make useful citizens.

'Squire Gray attends Court and looks on. He regrets that he made "that proposition," but the members of the Bar have taken no steps for his relief. He has a fondness for good securities and New England rum. If he can't practice law he can paint, and the bright blossom on his nose attests his proficiency. He tells strangers that he injured his voice pleading at the Bar. They look at his face and "guess the bar-keeper must have been very deaf."

Patience Wells is living with James and Bessie. She is tenderly cared for and fondly loved; but she cannot forget the past. There are wounds that Time cannot heal; wounds that Memory is ever probing; wounds that only Death can efface.

Lawyer Ainsworth is wearing the ermine. He is a just Judge, and enjoys, in a marked degree, the confidence of the whole people. He is a tried friend of James and Bessie Wells, and he spends many happy hours in their pleasant home. When he is not clear on a law point, he takes counsel of James, and his decisions are never reversed by a higher Court.

"Honest John" is still driving on the Glenville and Berwick stage route. He takes great pride in exhibiting a gold-mounted whip that was "presented by a gentleman as is a gentleman, from Novy Skoshy."

"I am so happy to-day, James."

"I trust you will always be happy, dear Bessie."

"This is one of the brightest of your 'compensations,' my dear niece."

"So it is, Uncle George."

"There is a knock at the door, James."

"I will answer it, if you will take this bundle of flannel, dear mother."

"Good morning, Mrs. Deford.   Come in."

"I can't stop, Jimmy.   Honest John is holdin' the stage for me.   I've brought you them stockins."